The Tickle Monster

E-Book ISBN: **979-8-9866624-5-9**
Paperback ISBN: **979-8-9866624-4-2**

Written By: David Washburn
Edited By: Kaylynn Wurzelbacher
Cover Design By: Tania at GetCovers.com
Published By: Burn Ward Publishing

This is a story inspired by the fun little games that parents play with their children while they still maintain their innocence. This is a tale about the closeness of a small family and the bonds that hold us together. Routines and rituals, learning and teaching one another in a time when you must depend on family. This is the story that twists those values and sinks the childhood innocence into the darkness. Into the darkness that only exists in places that children are told not to venture out to.

This is a work of fiction.

Instagram: @WashburnWrites
TikTok: @WashburnWrites
Email: DavidWritesStories@Gmail.com

First Edition
Edition: **1** 2 3 4 5 6 7 8 9

THE TICKLE MONSTER

A Novella

By

DAVID WASHBURN

CHAPTER ONE

Splinters of wood explode on impact as an arrow digs into a large tree from across a wooded terrain, at rapid speed. The fawn that the two teenage boys are tracking sprints away at the sound of danger as the arrow's tail sways with the momentum. "Dammit! Almost got it!" Abraham curses.

"You missed it by five feet, at least!" Jack replies with a hearty chuckle.

"I would've got 'em if that tree weren't in the way!" Abraham jogs over and extracts the arrow and slides it back into his belt loop with the others.

Jack walks ahead of Abraham, "Sure. Let's blame the trees," he taunts with a smirk.

Abraham jogs, taking light steps to catch up to Jack. "I don't see you hitting it either, Jacky."

Abraham and his friend Jack are wandering the woods near each of their homes. It is summertime in Massachusetts and nature is buzzing. Flowers bloom and are as fragrant as ever. The leaves on the trees are green and vibrant creating a canopy that hides the sun.

"My father made me this bow for my birthday, have a look," Jack says as he hands it to Abraham.

Abraham admires the wood finish and how smooth the wood is. "Yes, this is very nice, Jacky," he compliments as he tugs on the twine. "It's nice and tight." He hands it back to him.

Jack pulls an arrow from his belt and slots it against the string. He pulls slightly on it while aiming ahead at nothing in particular. "Yeah, but I was made to give my brother my old one though."

"He is what, ten?" Abraham asks, snickering.

Jack releases the tension and brings the bow to his side. "Yes. Father is eager to get him out here with us hunting birds and squirrels, I guess."

Abraham looks at his bow with chagrin, as he notices the cloth wrapping in the center of it is worn and unraveling. The notches that hold the string look like they have worn down enough for the string to slip off easily, and it could probably use a new string as well. "Lucky, I wish my father would give me a new bow."

"Don't be a sad sack, Abe. Yours works perfectly fine," Jack says with skepticism. "How long have you had that thing anyway?"

Abe pulls the head from a tall weed as they walk past it. He rolls the bud up between his index finger and thumb. "I don't know, since I was maybe nine."

"The only thing wrong with it is the trees then?" Jack replies.

"Well," Abraham begins, "I suppose it isn't the look of it, but how you use it."

"In that case, you're right," Jack says through a grin that pulls his lips to the side of his face.

"About what?"

"You do need a new bow then."

Abraham pushes Jack, playfully. "Shut up, ass."

Jack's laughter dies and his face becomes serious as he suddenly stops and holds his hand up, signaling for silence. Abraham stops moving and the boys are both on high alert. Jack turns his head and locks eyes with Abraham and he uses two fingers to point at his own eyes and in the direction not too far ahead of them. Abraham looks where Jack is pointing and he sees the fawn, with its head down eating from the floor of the woods. Jack sidesteps to get closer to Abraham. He leans over, "If I can bag this deer, you owe me a slice of your mother's apple pie," he whispers.

Abraham watches the fawn, a still target that is begging to be killed. Abraham holds out his hand. "Deal." Jack shakes and draws an arrow from his belt and slots it into the string.

Jack walks, light-footed, trying to avoid loud branches and dry leaves that might spook the deer. Jack leans against a large tree and drops a knee as he takes aim from about twenty-five feet away. With a big inhale, he holds his breath to steady his hands to try and get the perfect hit. The arrow is aimed just above this animal's head. Jack wants one shot to do the job. He releases and the moment he does, there is a noise that spooks the fawn to look up. The arrow makes contact with the deer, only scratching it, but enough to draw blood and scare it. The deer runs away.

"Shit!" Jack huffs.

Abraham snickers, "I guess that was better than a tree."

"Something spooked it!" Jack says, following a gasp.

"Well, that's a convenient excuse."

Jack jogs ahead, "Come on, Abe! We can't lose it!"

The boys are in pursuit of what might be an injured deer. Abraham is a few paces behind Jack when they hear a noise off in the distance. Something big, maybe. "What was tha-"

"Shhh!" Jack interrupts, holding his finger to his mouth.

The boys stand at full alert, and they see the fawn sprinting toward them, about twenty yards away. Jack spots it and stands upright with his bow drawn. The deer sees him and pivots, running in a different direction. Abraham gives chase now while Jack follows not far behind. As Abe closes the distance with the deer, they come into a clearing. The deer is out of sight and has shaken the boys. Abe hunches over with his hands on his knees, catching his breath. He is hit in the face with an overwhelming stench of death and rot that forces him to pull his arm over his nose. He buries down the urge to gag at the scent, breathing through his mouth. He hears Jack catch up to him as he stops beside him. Abraham looks up and takes in the scenery when he notices something on a tree. "Hey Jack," he says through a winded breath, "What's that?" he asks, pointing.

Jack's face changes as the smell hits him, "Oh, God! What is that smell!!?" he asks, covering his nose with the bend in his arm. His eyes follow Abraham's pointing finger where there is a large, red eye painted on the tree. He walks toward it, "I don't know. Some sort of weird finger painting?"

Abraham steps beside Jack, "Is it blood?" he asks.

Jack looks around, "I don't know. It's strange," he studies it closely for a moment. "It looks fresh though." He turns and looks up and notices sticks that are bundled in a peculiar arrangement that is not natural at all. Sticks overlapping in X patterns and some with a third stick that is straight and vertical that intersects the other two. They are twined together and hanging from the tree like some bizarre ornaments. Upon further studying, Jack notices tiny bones strung up like windchimes. Rodent skulls hang from the branches as well. "Have you ever seen anything like this before?" he asks, pointing above them.

Abraham looks up and before he could try to make sense of what he is seeing, he sees the fawn dashing through from his peripheral vision. Without a word, he darts off, determined to catch it. Abraham gives chase with an all-out effort, leaping over fallen trees, navigating bushes and low branches, and keeping it within sight. The deer stops eventually but Abraham is still a good distance from it. Maybe this is what he needs to get a shot off, uninterrupted. He quietly draws an arrow and readies his shot.

Abraham's hands are controlled and still with a gulp of air held in his lungs as he steadies the shot. *Breathe in…* He takes aim. It is perfect. The deer is still. An easy target. *This isn't even fair;* he arrogantly thinks to himself. He releases the string with an exhale, letting the wind guide the arrow as it pierces the deer's neck, just under its jaw. "Yes!" he shouts, rushing over to the fallen deer, eagerly, to confirm the kill. "Hey, Jacky! We talked about what I'd owe you, but we never talked about what you'd owe me if I got the kill," he says through a big grin. He pulls the arrow from the wound and wipes the blood off onto his pants. "What have you got to say about my shooting now?" Abraham stands and has a look around. "Jack… Come, look!"

Abraham slides the arrow into his belt and walks back toward the spot that he just saw Jack. "Come on, Jacky! You can't be that mad that you shoot your bow like a girl!" he taunts.

Abraham looks around in all directions unable to see Jack anywhere. "Jack!" he cries out, growing more concerned. "You better not be messing with me!"

Abraham hears a noise and turns back to find the deer, standing on all fours. In disbelief, he staggers backwards, watching the fawn and the blood that had run down its body, staining its coat. Abraham shudders at the sight of the deer he believed to have killed as it hops away, unbothered at all. He walks ahead and looks at the ground where it had fallen and sees nothing unusual. "Jack!" he calls out, once more to no answer. He hears sticks breaking and brush moving close by though. "Jack... Did you see the deer?" He hears the sounds again on the other side of him. He turns quickly to see nothing. The sound gets closer, alternating behind him each time he turns until finally he turns to see a woman standing in front of him.

Abraham becomes startled as she is so close that she is within reach of him. He lets out a scream that he stifles quickly, as she seems unthreatening. "Where did you come from?" he asks.

The pale-skinned woman wears black with trinkets hanging from her hair and neck. Her face is decorated with something dark, like blood; some sort of symbol Abraham has never seen before. She leans forward, her face within inches of Abraham's and she smiles, revealing a crude underbite and an awful mouthful of rotten teeth.

Before she can speak, Abraham sprints out so fast that he isn't worried about the deer anymore. He goes into survival mode and is no longer thinking about Jack. He hopes Jack is safe and just hiding somewhere messing with him. He escapes the woods that afternoon and Jack is not with him. Abraham begins to get scared at the thought that something awful might have happened.

Maybe Jack got lost. If he did though he would have heard Abraham calling. What if he got hurt and was knocked out somewhere? Is it possible Abraham got turned around and lost himself? Who was that woman? Abraham's brain is transitioning from worried to afraid as sunset is approaching.

Maybe Jack went home and was mad that Abraham got the kill. Maybe he didn't want to help him carry his trophy back home. How was that deer even still alive after taking an arrow through the neck? It is unlike Jack to throw a tantrum, but it isn't unheard of for someone to do. Thinking of what he is going to say to his parents, Abraham makes his way back home, without the deer, and without his friend.

Chapter Two

Twenty Years Later...

Teddy washes up for supper, making his dark, messy hair less messy than usual. He rinses his face and cleans his hands as he prepares to take his seat at the table with his family. Bickering with his younger sister Anna throughout the day has proved to be annoying but he has gotten through with her being a pest, like younger siblings can be. Despite her whining and brown-nosing with their mother, he is upbeat this evening. He has completed his reading for the day and now he waits for his father to come home from a day of hard work at the lumber yards outside of the ever-growing city of Boston, where they produce wood for boats, homes, ships, and many other things. Teddy has become bored with the books on religion that he has been reading about through the mornings that his mother has instructed that he read. His father Abraham has given him a book of fables that he has only dabbled with but is looking forward to reading and distancing himself from the preachy and matter-of-fact tones that come from books about religion.

"Ranger! Come on, boy!" Teddy hollers as he jogs out of the house and their dog jumps up wildly, excited to let out the pent-up energy as he follows him outside. His tongue hangs from his mouth as he pants, like he is smiling. His tail wags, knocking into furniture. Ranger is a friendly, English Pointer breed with white fur and large black spots on his body. Not a particularly big dog, but no runt either.

Teddy's mother Mary looks up at him as she sets the plates. "Teddy, put on your coat, you'll catch a chill."

He grabs his coat from the back of a chair on his way out. "I'm going to wait for father," he shouts with Ranger's nails tapping against the hardwood floor with each excited step, nearly tripping Teddy.

Mary has pulled out a smoked ham from the smokehouse out back and the entire household is excited for the meal. Sweet potatoes and a medley of peas and carrots decorate the table along with cornbread and a peach and plum jam that Anna has made all by herself for the first time yesterday that she is particularly proud of. The small home smells of a savory meal that has been prepared attentively since this morning.

Typical days look like this: Mary will wake up and prepare breakfast for her husband and the children. This usually would consist of leftovers from the night before. She would go to great lengths to waste nothing. Vegetables usually went into some sort of mush cake and that would be a simple enough breakfast. They happen to own a few hens as well, so they manage to gather eggs, but the hens only produce so much at a time. They have a goat that produces milk as well. Mary will then wake Abraham and the children, and they will all wash up and prepare for breakfast together at the table.

The family will see Abraham off to work for the day as he will have a little extra from breakfast to take with him. He will hug the children, hug his wife, and take his leave on horseback. The family will typically watch him ride off from the front door. After he has rode out of sight, Mary will tend to her duties as a mother and wife. She will first make sure Teddy has a lesson plan for the day, as education is important, and he is twelve years old and will be a man in no time. Once he is fully tasked, she will then have Anna follow her around like her little shadow. Anna helps clean the house and does basic chores and as the day goes on will help feed the hens, feed the goat, help with food preparations, and will sometimes go into town with Mary to run small errands. Following her mother's lead *is* her education.

Cambridge is a cold town in February, and today it wears an overcast sky that the sun can only whisper through. The air is cool under the gray clouds and silver linings. It's somehow beautiful and heavy all at once. Teddy leans against the goat pen's post, staring across the pasture where a skyline of trees make up the woods near their home. Teddy often finds himself studying these trees from a distance as the rowdy sense of adventure begs for him to explore what is beyond them. `What can his imagination make of the scenery from inside? He only daydreams of the possibility though because he has been disciplined in the past by his mother for wandering too far from the homestead. For as long as he can remember, he was always told not to veer too far from the house and to always be within shouting distance when he is called for. A house built on love isn't above having a strong hand across the bottom if this rule is disobeyed though, as his mother and father have long warned him and his little sister of coyotes and possibly other hungry animals in the woods. His mother would tell them if they wandered too far and got into trouble that they may not hear them scream if they were attacked. Their father is especially firm about this rule.

Teddy paces the dried-out dirt patch in front of the cottage-style home, kicking solid chunks of dirt and rocks with each step while Ranger circles his feet and playfully stands against him, starving for his attention. Teddy pushes him down and Ranger growls, bouncing around and Teddy gets low like the two are going to have it out. Ranger jumps first and Teddy puts him in a headlock and the two tumble to the ground. "I gotcha boy! I gotcha!" Teddy says excitedly while he struggles to restrain the energetic dog. "You're not going anywhere now!"

Ranger growls and gnaws on Teddy's forearm but not hard. Teddy laughs at him and lets him go and Ranger backs up for a second just before he pounces again. As the two are wrestling around, Ranger stops suddenly and faces the trees away from the house, studying something in that direction. Teddy watches, looking out while he catches his breath, and that's when he hears the galloping in the distance. The same galloping he has memorized and become conditioned to hearing everyday now, for years. Ranger takes off like a pebble from a slingshot toward the sound and Teddy sees his father approaching from the distance.

Ranger runs alongside Abraham and the horse as they ride up to the house. Teddy waits as Abraham climbs down and pulls his satchel from the harness. "Hey there, Teddy," he greets.

"Hello, sir," Teddy replies.

"How's it going, son?" Abraham asks.

"Good."

Abraham looks around the front of the house, noticing the hen house with the calm chickens, and the pen where the goat paces in an enclosed area. He walks the horse into a small fenced-in pasture with a small shelter that comes off the side of the house. After he has situated the animals, he steps inside of his humble, small farm cottage. As he closes the front door he is greeted with the wonderful smells of smoked meat and cooked vegetables that waft through the house.

"Father!" Anna shouts as she runs up to him and throws her arms around his waist tight.

"Hey, hey Anna," he says, trying to walk, but restricted to smaller strides with her arms squeezing him. He shuffles over to Mary who has just about finished setting the table, leans over and plants a kiss on her lips. "Hey, honey."

"Welcome home, dear," she says as she wipes her hands onto a rag.

"Smells great! You all must have been busy today," Abraham notices.

Mary smiles sweetly, "Well, the vegetables were just something I threw together, but the ham is perfect." Her eyes meet Abraham's and she looks at the jam on the table and then nods her head toward Anna, who isn't aware. Abraham looks surprised as he catches onto what Mary is hinting at.

"Oh... Oh, and *what* is that sweet, sweet smell? I can't quite figure it out," Abraham asks, trying to hide his amusement with a smile that peeks out of the corner of his mouth.

"It's my jam, father!" Anna says proudly, jogging around the table to present it to her father with a smile and both hands outstretched showcasing her divine contribution to supper this evening.

"Oh, wow! You made this?" he asks as he dips his finger in it and has a taste. Much to his surprise it was actually very good. "I'm impressed Anna, good job sweetheart!" he licks his finger clean of any sweetness on his fingertip, "Mmm *Mmm*."

Like most days, the family engages in their routines. Most being just as predictable as the last, with interchangeable ingredients to the days. Abraham comes home, they wash up for supper, Abraham says a prayer before the meal, and then they sit down for the meal together as a family. They all eat and talk about their days. Abraham talks about his workday in the lumber yards, Mary talks about the children's studies and what was done around the house, tending to the animals and such. Teddy feeds scraps to Ranger under the table even though his mother has asked him not to, many times over, and Anna watches anxiously as everyone tries her jam. It is a hit with the family and she is walking on clouds because of it.

After supper Mary asks Anna to help her clean up the table while Abraham asks Teddy to meet him out back. Teddy grabs his coat and Ranger follows him out the door. It grows a little colder and the already hidden sun falls beyond the horizon while Teddy meets his father in the increasing darkness. Abraham is near a flat tree stump where they regularly split wood for cooking and warmth inside. Abraham has an ax and has already begun going to work. "Set it up," he orders Teddy, motioning at the large piece of wood for Teddy to set carefully for him to split it. Teddy does as he is asked quickly and as he backs away, the ax slams down, splitting the wood with ease. Teddy sets up another, and this goes on for a few moments, one after the next. Teddy sets the next piece and gathers the split pieces into a neat pile at the foot of the tree stump.

"Father," Teddy mutters, "may I try?"

Abraham looks at the ax for a moment and then at Teddy. "Well… I don't see why not," he says before he plants the heavy head of the ax into the edge on the tree stump. Teddy's face lights up as he is a little surprised. He half-expected his father to say no, as he usually does with certain things that have to do with tending to the land. "Go on, have at it." his father encourages.

Abraham leans against a wooden post with Ranger lying at his feet, watching his first-born son grab the handle of the ax and give it a tug with all he has. "Grrrr Aggh!" Teddy roars as he fails to remove the ax.

Discouragement is written on Teddy's red face and heavy breathing. Abraham smirks as he walks over. "Son," Abraham says, gripping the handle of the ax by the neck, "You struggled, because you were trying to drag the blade further into the trunk." He pulls on the handle to demonstrate. "You have to pivot the handle up to free the wedge," he says as he raises the handle high. Teddy stares at the blade moving incrementally within the tree. "And once you've done it like this," he pulls the ax free from the stump with ease, "the ax should come free." He hands the ax to Teddy, who takes it with both hands, admiring his father's ease of strength. Abraham grabs a piece of wood and places it onto the stump, where it awaits the splitting justice that Teddy hopes to dish out.

Teddy watches his father as he raises the ax. Abraham grins proudly and gives a nod. Teddy looks at the wood, lines up his tool and raises the ax above his head and brings it down into the wood. The ax hits the wood, but it escapes on contact and bounces into some dirt near the pile of split wood. Teddy exhales, frustrated, "I think it's too heavy," he suggests.

"That's okay, you're still a growing boy," Abraham says as he places the wood back on the stump. "You've got plenty of time to pack on muscle." Teddy rears back and takes another, less concentrated swing with a big boy grunt... And misses the wood entirely. "Let me show you son."

"It's too heavy!" Teddy complains.

Abraham stands behind him. "Face the wood, son." He adjusts Teddy's hands at much better positions to control the counterbalance of the ax. "See, what you're doing is swinging with your arms when you need to be using your entire body. Stiffen your shoulders... Control your hands, and step into it the next time you swing it. Line it up like you've been doing, but step into your swing this time."

"Yes, sir," Teddy responds firmly. He closes his eyes and takes a deep breath.

Abraham steps back. "Whenever you're ready, son."

Teddy opens his eyes and just like his father instructed him to do, he lines it up, controls his hands, and raises the ax, and this time he steps into his swing. He notices immediately that it is much easier, and he feels ten times stronger as the ax glides down and sends the wood onto the ground, accompanied by that satisfying sound on both sides of the tree. The head of the ax sticks into the trunk a little and Teddy's eyes light up. "Yes! I did it!"

"Yes, you did son," Abraham agrees, placing his hands on Teddy's shoulders. "Great work! I'm very proud of you son."

Teddy pulls the ax from the stump, this time, easily, just like his father showed him. He leans the ax against the stump and races to gather both pieces of wood from the ground. "Can I do another?" he asks with reignited enthusiasm.

Abraham smiles bigger, "Sure, go on, son."

Teddy adds the wood pieces to the growing pile and then picks the ax up. His father places a new chunk of wood. He lines up the ax and prepares to chop.

"Teddy... Soon, I'm going to have to show you some things."

Teddy chops the wood and is grinning big. "Like what?"

Abraham places another piece of wood on the stump. "Well, for one, how to handle yourself." Abraham steps back, "You're going to be a man soon and with that people are going to expect things of you."

Teddy prepares his next swing. "What kind of things?"

"Well," Abraham starts as Teddy swings the ax and the wood splits in two, "You'll have to know how to handle yourself... How to do more around here..."

Teddy rests the ax on his shoulder while he listens, "Yes, sir."

Abraham picks up the split pieces off the ground. "And second, you're going to have to look out for your mother and sister when I'm not around."

"I already do look out for 'em," Teddy replies.

Abraham snickers, "I know you do, but you're a boy still and there is only so much you can– Never mind, that's beside the point. I'm just sayin' that I'm gonna show you some more things."

"Yes, sir," Teddy replies like the energy was sapped out of him as he goes to set up another piece of wood.

"That's enough. I think we have plenty for tonight and tomorrow," Abraham says. Teddy swings the ax and drives it into the stump, the same way that his father had it when they started. "And the third, and final thing, and I want you to really listen to me here," he places a hand on Teddy's shoulder and looks him in the eye, and then his eyes look up toward the trees at the edge of the property, with two fingers pointing out. "Never go into those woods."

Teddy looks out to the trees along the far edge of the yard. He studies the leafless trees in the distance with confusion. "How come?"

Abraham looks down at him and smirks. "Well, what version do you want me to tell you? The version I would tell *my boy* Teddy? Or… The version I can trust, *the man* Teddy with?"

Teddy looks up at him and smiles, "Tell me the truth, father."

Abraham sighs, "All right then," he huffs as he sits on the tree trunk, crosses his arms and stares out at the sky. Teddy leans against the tree trunk and Ranger comes up to him and sits beside him. "I used to have a best friend when I was a boy. Jack was his name. We were thick as thieves; I'd say I was thirteen or fourteen. We were playing, running amok, when we wandered off into those woods… That day, we saw something that frightened us both. So much so that I believe I may have even screamed. I don't remember much from that moment, but I remember running as fast as I could, and I got the hell out of those woods. When I got out, I turned around finally, and my friend was not behind me. He was gone."

Teddy's eyes stare into his father's in disbelief. "What was out there?"

Abraham looks at him with dramatic pause. "Just don't go into the woods, son."

CHAPTER THREE

Teddy and his father finish gathering wood and make their way back into their home. Ranger follows them inside where Teddy takes the wood to the fire that Mary has already started. She stands up after adding a couple of logs to the fire, "Anna, Teddy, why don't you two clean up and get yourselves ready for bedtime?"

"Yes, mother," Anna responds.

"Father let me cut the wood!" Teddy says, lighting up with pride.

Mary places her hand on Teddy's cheek, lovingly, with a wide, thin-lipped smile, "That's great, dear," she says, adoring him proudly, "go get washed up now."

"Yes, mother," Teddy replies.

As the children go off and clean themselves up, Mary finishes up the chores around the house. Abraham changes out of his work clothes and gets himself prepared for sleep. The children change into sleep clothes and go to their room where they wait for their parents to come and tell them goodnight. Typically, Anna and Teddy will talk and do things to irritate one another at this time.

After a while, Abraham will creep into their room, and he will talk with them both. He starts with Anna and sits on the edge of her bed. He asks about her day and what she learned. She will ask him about his day at the lumberyard and the docks and if he saw any big ships. He tells her fantastical stories of massive vessels and what he does to make sure they are safe to venture up and down the coast. Anna's face is always awestruck whenever he tells her about the ships, as she has a fascination for the water. This goes on for a bit before Mary comes in and sits beside Teddy. Mary will tell him how much she loves him, and he will echo the same to her. She tells him how proud of him she is regularly. He tells her that he knows.

"...And then a naval vessel came by and docked," Abraham says to Anna.

"What were the navy men doing?" Anna asks softly.

"Well, I suppose they were here to protect us," he says with a sideways smirk on his face.

Anna gazes into his eyes with a bashful smile, "What are they protecting us from?"

"Well," he begins, as he raises his hands up, wiggling his fingers, "I guess they are here to save you from the Tickle Monster!" Abraham begins to tickle Anna's tummy and as fast as her hands go to stop him, his hands move quickly to her underarms. She wriggles around, flopping and jerking away from him with a burst of laughter.

She kicks and kicks as she tries to get out the words to tell him to stop but the involuntary laughter drowns out any chance of getting a word out.

"What's that? You want me to... Start?"

"No! St-" she cannot get the words out, but Abraham pretends he doesn't know, while he continues to tickle her.

"You want me to... Stay?" he lets up for a moment so she can catch her breath.

"No" she says with flushed cheeks, a big smile, and winded breath. "*Stop!*"

Abraham smiles at her and adjusts her blanket. "Okay, okay... I am done tickling *you*," he says as his head slowly turns toward Teddy.

Teddy looks over at him and knows what is about to happen, so he tenses up.

Abraham stands up and shows his hands like he is a monster, fingers wagging in all different directions, "Gitchy gitchy *goo*, *I'm* gonna tickle *you*," he sings in a silly voice.

Anna pulls the cover over her head with a shriek.

Mary stands up from Teddy's bed with her eyes open-wide, shooting daggers through Abraham.

With his hands still in the playful, mangled position he catches Mary's eyes. "What?"

"You know that Anna doesn't like when you do that voice." Mary reminds him.

Teddy laughs at Anna, like he does every time whenever she gets scared of father's Tickle Monster voice.

Abraham turns to Anna, "I'm sorry sweetheart," and then he turns back to Teddy, "and what are you laughing at, young man!?" he shouts, leaping onto Teddy's bed as he begins to tickle him, but a little rougher than he had done with Anna.

With Abraham's probing fingers landing between Teddy's ribs and crawling across his body to his many other ticklish places, Teddy is a kicking, squirming, ball of laughter. The kicking is much more forceful than when Anna was kicking and like most nights, this little nighttime ritual starts with tickling and ends with the *men of the house* rough-housing and wrestling on the floor.

The two wrestle in Teddy's bed until Teddy gets free and stands up on the floor. His bare feet move across the floor as he gets into a defensive position. "Ah, someone's feeling brave I see," Abraham says in the Tickle Monster voice.

"Alright now, boys," Mary says.

Abraham lunges at Teddy and grabs him, slamming him onto his bed. Teddy lands softly onto his back but manages to put his father in a headlock, trapping him.

Mary looks over at Anna and speaks to her with just facial expressions, as she looks at Abraham, exposed with his back to the room as Teddy holds him. Anna smiles big and jumps up from her bed. "Tickle your father!" Mary cries out as she and Anna begin to tickle a trapped Abraham. Laughter and the joyful sounds of a close family fill the room as Anna's infectious and innocent high-pitch giggling is the percussion to everyone else's happiness. Abraham is able to get to his feet while simultaneously lifting Teddy up from the bed and is able to free himself from Teddy's headlock.

Abraham reaches back and grabs Anna. "Who is this I've got? Who is this?" he says playfully. Before he can even get a chance to tickle her, she slips away and runs out of the bedroom laughing.

"Alright, alright." Mary says, attempting to bring order to bedtime, "Abraham, you're going to get them all riled up and they're never going to get any sleep."

Teddy sits up in his bed with a smile for his parents while Abraham groans as he gets himself upright to his feet. "I suppose Mother is right," Abraham says as he leans in for a hug to Teddy, "I guess the Tickle Monster will have to come back another night." Anna stands in the doorway with a bashful grin carved into her face, accompanied by a giggle. "Get over here my little bug!" he says with his arms wide as he lowers to a single knee. Anna tackles him and squeezes him tightly. It's less of a hug and more of her testing her strength to see how hard she can squeeze before he gives in for her to stop. Abraham makes a silly face like he's choking, and Anna lets go, pleased with her rouse. "You got me, dear... But it's time for you to get some sleep, young lady," he says as he explodes to his feet, snatching her in one swift movement and he lays her to bed gently. She shuffles her feet into the covers and Abraham tucks her in.

"I love you, Father," Anna says just before she lets out a big yawn. Mary has a seat at her bedside, and tucks her in, and kisses her forehead. "I love you, Mother,"

Mary smiles with flushed cheeks. "Good night sweetie. I love you too,"

Anna closes her eyes and the parents go to Teddy's bed now, where he lies grinning at Abraham, expecting more bedtime games.

"You get some sleep now," Abraham says to him, as he goes in for a hug, "Make sure you protect your sister *from the Tickle Monster.*"

Mary gives a playful slap to Abraham as he stands upright and backs away from the bed. She sits beside Teddy and puts a hand on his face and smiles. "I love you Teddy,"

"Goodnight, Mother," he responds.

Mary stands and as she and Abraham make their way out of the room, Mary grabs the oil lantern and blows it out as Abraham pulls the door closed. Teddy lies in bed and makes himself comfortable facing Anna, who lies quiet. Like most nights, he lies in bed staring at the walls, with just his thoughts to keep him awake as he reflects on his day. On this night he thinks about what his father had told him earlier, about becoming a man soon. He was eager to one day be able to *be more,* but he also still felt very much like a boy in his heart. He studies the moonlight shining into their room through the single small window, and how it casts shadows on the wall from the leafless trees of Winter. They lend their projections to their bedroom and the wind sings a song while the branch's shadows dance and sway until Teddy drifts off to sleep.

The following afternoon, after a morning of arithmetic for Teddy and helping mother with laundry for Anna, the two siblings find themselves outside with Ranger playing. The air is cool as the clouds create a palisade that does well to hide the sun from their small little world. Ranger has a stick in his mouth, a perfect one for throwing, that he is returning to Anna. "Good boy, Ranger!" she shouts with glee. Ranger drops the stick at her feet and barks at her picking up the stick.

"That was good," Teddy begins, "but I can throw it farther."

Anna's face twists with doubt. "Nuh uh, prove it," she demands as she hands Teddy the stick and Ranger raises up onto his hind legs with his panting tongue and wagging tail, watching the stick intently.

"Okay," Teddy takes the stick, "watch the professional." He takes a couple of large strides back and stretches his arms across his body and then outward. Ranger drops his front-end low to the ground with his hind end up as he barks, waiting for what comes next. Teddy takes several massive strides, almost like a running start, as he whips the stick across his body and sends it spinning across the land. Anna's eyes widen as she gasps in disbelief. Ranger bursts like a greyhound the moment Teddy even acts like he is going to throw. Ranger glides through the lot over spotty patches of grass and weeds and the stick hurling over him and ahead.

"No fair! You had a running start," Anna cries.

"How is that not fair?" Teddy replies defensively.

Anna stomps her foot, "I didn't get a good throw."

Teddy shrugs with his hands outstretched, "Well, there are no rules saying you couldn't have."

Anna sighs as she looks out at Ranger. "Teddy?"

"Yes?"

"Ranger ran into the woods."

"Oh no," Teddy says, with a sense of dread driving his tone. "Ranger! ... Come 'ere boy!"

Anna immediately becomes panicked at Teddy's expression. "Ranger! ... Come back here!"

"Ranger!" Teddy cries out again. He puts two fingers between his lips and whistles loud.

"Why did he run off? He never runs off!" Anna asks.

"I'm not sure," Teddy responds as he looks out to the trees.

"You have to go get him," Anna begs.

He looks at her like she is crazy, "Why do I have to go get him?"

Anna puts her hands on her waist and slams her foot down, "Because, you're a *boy,*" she responds assertively.

"That's ridiculous," Teddy commands. "Father told me last night not to go into the woods."

"Why would he say that?"

"He did not say, he just said it like it was dangerous, maybe."

"Well, you're going to have to," Anna says with no concern for her father's rules, only the dog.

"But it was you who played the stupid game with the stick," Teddy argues.

"But you threw the stick!" she huffs.

"Ranger!" Teddy calls out again to no reaction.

"Please, Teddy," Anna says with her eyes welling up.

Teddy hangs his head low as the rest of his body sags. He considers for a moment telling their mother but she is busy tending to the housework and he never wants to be a bother if he can help it. He also sees that his little sister is hurting and upset about their dog mysteriously vanishing off into the trees that are about fifty yards away from the side of the house. *Last night Father said I would be a man soon and that I would need to look out for my mother and sister when he is not around,* Teddy justifies.

"Fine… I'll go," Teddy says with a sigh.

"Be careful," Anna tells him.

"Yeah," he says reluctantly.

Teddy walks away from Anna, leaving her standing there worried. He picks up his pace and it becomes a jog as he makes his way into the trees. Teddy has now gone into the woods.

Chapter Four

Teddy steps into the woods and crossing over the earthy threshold feels strange to him. Strange now because it is forbidden. As he looks around, he is filled with thrill like any boy his age might be, but it is also misguided under the circumstances. He wonders how come he has never played in the woods up until this point, even when he was outside alone, the thought had never occurred to him. Perhaps he was always too preoccupied with whatever he was being asked to do. He doesn't recall a time ever of being told not to go into the woods before his father asked him not to, but he also recalls times where his mother would tell him to watch his sister, or not to wander off. Perhaps that was Mary's way of not having to set a boundary while keeping them close by.

Completely ensnared with the trees from inside the woods, Teddy continues to call out for Ranger. The trees surround him and the more steps he takes into the woods, the darker it begins to feel. The musky-sweet aroma of crunchy fall leaves dance on the cool air, sneaking into his nose.

"Ranger," he hollers, followed by whistling. He doesn't hear a response at all but there are sounds of birds above him, chirping. Aside from that, it is quiet. He turns around and realizes how far into the woods he is now, as he cannot see out of the woods in any direction. He swallows the sudden lump in his throat as he tries to wear a brave face. Onward Teddy marches, with the trees practically on top of him. He climbs over a fallen pine tree and maneuvers through the brush that obstructs any sort of path at all. The sounds subtly become more removed from the moment and now the quiet is only magnified more by the trees growing closer together with each step, and the darkness becoming even deeper and deeper with every breath.

Teddy notices all of this but doesn't find it alarming, as he has never been in the woods. He is not afraid, only afraid of what sort of trouble Ranger must have got himself into. Did Ranger go chasing after a rabbit? Did something scare him away? Ranger has never done this before, in the middle of play no less. As Teddy continues his traverse through, the quiet is shattered by a distant barking sound.

"Ranger!" he calls out. He hears the barking, ongoing and he picks up his pace in the direction of the sound. "Ranger!" he cries out once more. Through the trees and dense, north-eastern wilderness that swallows him up, he pushes forward with his heart pounding, so much that he can feel his heartbeat in his ears, banging like a war drum. The barks are closer and closer and as he looks ahead, he sees a small cottage in the middle of the woods. Smoke billows from a small chimney stack. *Is someone living out here?* he wonders. The small cottage sits practically camouflage into the backdrop of nature. Earth colors from dirt and rocks. Moss growing at the base and vines climbing up the visible side of the structure. He notices as he gets closer to this cottage that the smell of dead leaves is overwhelmed with the sudden smell of something putrid. Decay and rot linger in the air, and it causes Teddy to wince as he brings his arm to his nose.

"Ranger!" he shouts another time. The bark is closer and as he studies the cottage during his approach, he sees a clearing around the front of the cottage, and that is when he sees Ranger. "Hey boy!" he shouts, but Ranger is being held by a woman, crouched on one knee, holding Ranger closely against her. His tail wags and he cranes his neck up to try and lick her face. "Um, excuse me, miss... That's my dog," he proclaims, still trying to cover his nose as he stumbles over his words.

The woman is unmoved by his words as she slowly pets Ranger for a moment longer. Her skin is pale but weathered with age. Her hair is long and black, much like the dress she is wearing. She raises her head slowly and her eyes meet Teddy's and at that moment he is overtaken with nerves. Her face is paler than her hands and she has dark eyes that feel like she is staring through him. Her face bears red markings across her cheekbones, just under her eyes and she wears many necklaces with different pendants. Some pendants look like small bones. Teddy thinks that she reminds him of one of their native friends from the city, only more unsettling.

"Ranger... Come on boy," he calls out, with a less than enthusiastic tone now. Ranger tries to come to him, but she jerks him closer to her again, continuing to stroke his fur while holding eye contact. Teddy observes the surroundings, mainly the cottage, and he sees dreamcatchers hanging over the front door from the stoop. Bundles of sticks are tied and placed at the corners of the cottage and there are flat stones stacked on the ground in several places visible from where he is standing.

"That's my dog ma'am," Teddy says with a hand extended, "I can take him back now."

Ranger barks as he enjoys being loved on. The woman blinks for the first time, her eyes not quite in sync with one another. One eyelid is just a bit slower than the other. "You ought to not wander into the woods, boy."

Teddy takes small steps toward her, as he can hardly hear her voice. He can hear it just well enough to know it is strained and gravely. "I- I just- I just came to- to get my dog," he falters.

The woman holds Ranger longer, tilting her head slowly to the side, continuing to stare through Teddy. "You would do well to mind your beast, *boy*," she suggests, but *this* felt more like a warning. Teddy notices the points in her teeth as she speaks, like they had been filed to a point. A mouthful of browned and pointed teeth spewing venom disguised as a pleasantry.

"Let him go," Teddy says, with a boyish bravado.

"I do not like when visitors come into my woods. I do not take well to surprises," she snaps.

"I'm sorry, I didn't know."

"You should listen to your father, Teddy," she warns.

"How... H-how do you know my name?"

She strokes Ranger, more aggressively as she stares at Teddy, tilting her head to the other side. "Your father told you not to go into the woods, *boy*."

"Who are you?" Teddy asks, becoming agitated and scared.

The woman tilts her head slowly to the other side, "I *am* the woods, I am the trees, I am the roots in the darkness that sprout in your dreams."

Teddy feels the cold prickling fingers of the winter crawling up his spine as she says that like a playful nursery rhyme. "Just give me back my dog, and we will go."

Teddy stands firm, growing more and more anxious as a shroud of darkness descends onto the tree canopy and the trees feel more and more close. Ranger is just a few steps away, but when he barks, his bark is only heard like it would be from a much longer distance. Teddy has a sinking feeling in his body, like he is falling away from his body, and the trees are on top of him. The woman's words, *I am the woods,* bounce around his brain, like an echo that won't stop. He stares ahead still despite this feeling, watching her holding onto Ranger tighter, and tighter, until his barking becomes a struggling yelp.

"Go now, boy..." she says very menacingly, showing her clenching teeth as she releases Ranger and rises to her feet. "Run," she hisses in her gravelly voice. "Run... Run..." as she repeats the command, her voice multiplies in Teddy's brain, like a devilish choir carrying a warning. The word repeats and each time the pitch drops deeper until it is unrecognizable speech. Teddy stands frozen, and stunned, unsure what he was just a part of when the chanting morphs into his name.

"Teddy... Teddy... Teddy..." the pitch raises with each time he hears his name and becomes closer until he is suddenly able to move his legs and he hears Anna's voice calling his name, with urgency.

"Teddy!" she cries. Teddy feels something licking his face and something tugging on his coat sleeve. "Teddy! Teddy, wake up! Come on!" she screams, hysterical with tears.

He opens his eyes with Ranger licking him, and he sees Anna beside him trying to pull him to his feet. "Stop! I'm getting up," he says, jerking his arm away from her. Everything feels normal again. The trees, no longer on top of him. No looming sense of dread or darkness creeping from above.

"Why were you out here sleeping?"

"I wasn't sleeping, I-"

"You were just lying on the ground sleeping. I got scared and came in behind you after a couple minutes when you didn't call back to me."

Teddy looks around very confused, but he doesn't tell her about what happened, as it doesn't exactly make sense to him either. There is no woman in black anywhere to be found, and no signs of a cottage in the middle of the woods. The longer he is on his feet, the more certain he is that it was a dream. Ranger trots along at his feet as they make their way out of the woods.

Chapter Five

Anna and Teddy come out of the woods with Ranger trotting ahead of them. He keeps stopping and looking back at them to make sure they're nearby while Anna asks a million questions.

"Did something happen before I found you?"

"No," Teddy huffs, "...I don't think so,"

Anna skips ahead and begins to keep pace, walking backwards, "Where was Ranger?"

"I'm not sure, I hadn't found him before I blacked out," Teddy answers, annoyed.

"Aha! So you were sleeping!?" Anna determines.

Teddy rolls his eyes, "I wasn't sleeping."

"You weren't answering when I called your name, and you looked sleepy when I woke you up."

Ranger grabs a stick and marches over to Teddy to deliver it to him. "Not right now," Teddy snaps.

Ranger takes the stick to Anna and climbs up her side. She takes the stick from him and stops for a moment and stretches, much like she had seen Teddy do earlier in the afternoon. She takes a few running strides and throws the stick overhand, sending it sailing toward the house. "Go get it boy!" she shouts. Ranger explodes like an arrow fired from a tight string. Anna watches the stick spinning through the air proudly. She begins to jog ahead of Teddy. "Come on, Teddy!"

Teddy continues walking, unbothered by her. He is exhausted and just wants to go inside now. He gets to the house moments after Anna and Ranger have already gone inside. As he walks into the front door, Anna is taking her shoes off as she is talking to their mother. Mary seems to be in the middle of doing something with some corn husks on the dinner table. They appear to be freshly picked.

"...and then Teddy went next, and he threw the stick really really far. So far it went into the woods," Anna says, talking almost too quickly to understand in all her excitement.

Mary listens with a pleasant smile on her face, "That's great dear."

"Yeah, and then Ranger went after the stick, but then ran past the stick, and he ran into the woods," Anna continues as Mary's smiling face becomes an expression much more attentive and concerned, "and then we were calling for Ranger, but he didn't come back, and then Teddy whistled, and he still did not come back,"

"Is Ranger okay?" Mary asks, with her eyes darting back and forth from Anna and Ranger.

"Yes, Mother. Ranger is okay, Teddy went to go get him?"

"What do you mean? Teddy had gone into the woods?"

"Yes."

Mary storms over to Teddy as he is dressing down and she hugs him. "Oh my, son, are you alright?"

Teddy stands confused and completely caught off-guard. "I am fine, Mother."

"Had your father not told you not to go into the woods?" Mary asks.

"He had, Mother. It was Anna who begged me to go after him," Teddy says, gesturing to Ranger who lies happily on the floor.

Mary looks at Anna who looks offended that Teddy would blame her. "I was afraid of the woods, Mother. I was scared that Ranger might never come back," Anna cries.

Mary takes a deep breath and exhales, still close to Teddy. "I'm just glad you two are alright. No more playing in the woods."

"Teddy fell asleep in the woods," Anna adds.

Mary hesitates for a moment as the pieces come together, "What do you mean *fell asleep*?"

"Be quiet Anna, you don't know what you're talking about," Teddy fires at Anna.

"What do you mean he fell asleep, Anna?" Mary repeats more urgently.

"I *mean* I went after him to look after I yelled for him and I found him lying on the ground, in the woods, sleeping," Anna explains.

"Teddy… What happened in the woods?" Mary interrogates, firmly.

"Nothing, I think I just passed out while I was looking for Ranger," he replies.

Mary stands in front of Teddy with a hand on his shoulder, and a hand on her forehead. She is seething. "People don't just *pass out* in the woods Teddy!" Mary hunches over, face to face with Teddy, pointing an authoritative finger in his face. "Listen to me... You are to *never* go into those woods again," she says with a look that blurs the thin line between angry and frightened. "Do you understand?"

"Yes, Mother. I'm sorry," Teddy says, completely deflated.

Mary fixes herself upright and looks at Anna and back at Teddy. "Ranger would have come home, I assure you." The children are silent after being scolded by their mother. "Anna, I will need your help with supper. Your father will be home soon, and we would be wise to have supper prepared before he hears of the trouble you two have made."

"Yes, Mother," Anna says with her voice muffled by her shame.

"Teddy, you have chores I believe. I suggest you get to it," Mary reminds him.

"Yes, Mother," he says, sulking.

Later in the afternoon Abraham arrives home from another day at the lumber yards. He comes into the house and Anna is quiet as she helps Mary set the table for supper. The smell of smoked ham fills the home, and apple cider simmers in a pot over a fire.

Abraham takes a whiff, "Mmmm, smells wonderful, dear."

"Thank you, supper will be ready in just a few moments," Mary says as she comes over to Abraham and kisses him on the cheek as he dresses down. "Why don't you get cleaned up and it will be ready when you come back."

"Thank you, dear," Abraham says. Anna is helping her mother tend to supper. Abraham greets her, "Hello, Anna."

"Hello, Father," she replies softly, as she sets plates onto the table, avoiding eye contact with him.

Abraham removes his boots and carries them in one hand and his coat in his other. He looks at Mary, who meets his glance and says nothing. He watches Anna, setting the table, waiting for her to look up but she never does. "What's going on?"

Anna's eyes meet his as she hesitates, "Earlier today we—"

"At at at!" Mary interrupts, "We will discuss this after supper, let your father settle in, dear."

Teddy is outside, behind the house, isolating, sitting on a tree trunk. He is snapping off pieces of a stem from a tall weed into tiny pieces while he sits anxiously awaiting his father to come home. His mother reacted angrily when she heard of him going into the woods. He wondered what it was exactly that his parents were not telling him. Teddy has begun to put the pieces together to what he knows. His father told him of when he was a child and went into the woods but didn't say much more than that his friend came out changed somehow.

The woman in the woods with the old cottage was something he couldn't stop thinking about. He did not understand what it was exactly he had seen, or if he had actually seen it or not. It all felt so real but he clearly passed out at some point. He had felt completely fine going into the woods before that had happened. He feels fine right now. Ranger was safe and seemed unphased by anything. Teddy continued to shred another weed, more aggressively now, dropping them at his feet and around the base of the tree stump. He anticipates a punishment but is upset at the point of not understanding why he is to be punished. Why is he not supposed to go into the woods? Why did his mother's voice sound angry but her face looked afraid before scolding him? He wonders what is beyond those trees that his father and mother do not want him to know about. Parents have a way of lying to kids, thinking that they are protecting them, but only provoking a natural, and at times rebellious curiosity.

"Teddy… Supper is ready," Mary calls out. "Come wash up."

Teddy stands and brushes the shredded weeds from his lap and makes the slow walk back into the house. As he comes in, he sees Anna standing near the table, Mary bringing a pan to the table with the ham in it, and Abraham has already taken his seat. "Hey there, Teddy," Abraham says from the table.

"Hello, Father," he replies, passing the table as he makes his way to the washroom to clean up.

Teddy washes his face and cleans his hands, comes out of the washroom with an appetite that clashes with a nervous belly. He has had a few hours to simmer about this.

"May I be seated, Father?" Anna asks.

Abraham gestures his hand toward her chair, "Please, have a seat."

Mary folds a worn-out rag and places it on a shelf and has a seat across from Abraham. Teddy stands in the room, so far into his own thoughts that he doesn't hear his father speaking to him.

"Teddy!" Abraham shouts. Teddy snaps out of it, and visibly shakes it off. "What's going on with you, boy? Are you not feeling well?"

"Sorry, I-" Teddy says, reaching for the words that escape him.

"Come, sit," Abraham tells him, gesturing for his seat. Teddy seats himself, across from Anna. Mary extends her hands to Teddy and Anna, and they each take a hand, and they extend their opposite hands to their father. They all join hands, bow their heads, and pray for their meal.

They say *amen* collectively. Mary reaches for a dish with a vegetable medley in it while Abraham slices the ham into thick cuts. "So," Mary begins, "Tell us about your day, dear," she says, eyeing Abraham.

Abraham distributes ham slices onto the children's plates and then Mary asks Teddy to pass her plate to his father. "Well, today was a spectacle, if I do say so myself," Abraham says, as he puts ham onto a plate and passes to Teddy, who passes back to his mother.

"What do you mean?" Mary asks.

The children have begun eating their food already. Abraham begins to slice his ham into bite size chunks. "Well, a gentry fellow arrived on the docks, one who seems to be the new man in charge," Abraham takes a bite and slices his next piece while he is chewing.

"Oh, a new boss. Is this good?" Mary asks, while she takes a sip of apple cider.

"Says he is from Cambridge and will be overseeing the ports. Import, export, quite tedious matters."

"Oh, that is interesting, Abe," Mary says, "Does this mean anything for you?"

Abraham swallows a bite and wipes his mouth on a cloth, "Hard to say yet. Could go either way. Some of the other workers don't seem too pleased at all."

Mary looks at Anna, "Dear, tell your father what we did this morning."

"We started to dry some apples!" she says, proudly.

"Oh, that is fantastic. I love apples," Abraham says, with a mouthful of vegetables.

"She is becoming quite the little helper around here," Mary says, looking at Anna with a grin.

Abraham puts his eyes on Teddy, "What about you Teddy? What did you study today?"

Teddy pushes a single pea around his plate with his fork. "... Arithmetic."

Abraham smirks and looks around the table, "Well, you ought not sound excited about it," he says with a dash of sarcasm.

"Teddy might not be feeling much like his chipper self," Mary observes.

"Why is that?" Abraham asks.

Mary wipes her mouth with a cloth, "Well," she takes a sip of the cider and sets the cup down. "Teddy disobeyed a simple rule, and I'm sure he is a little embarrassed."

Abraham looks at Teddy and sets his fork and knife on the table. The wooden chair cries against the shifting weight as he leans back. "What did you do Teddy?"

Teddy takes a deep breath, preparing to speak.

"He went into the woods today." Anna spills, before he could even get a word out.

Teddy looks at Anna with an expression that is universally understood to *stop talking*.

Abraham's voice has become more serious, and matches his face, "... You went into the woods today?"

Teddy hangs his head low, his shame evident, "Yes sir," Abraham sits quietly for a moment, measuring his reaction as he eyes Teddy. Teddy feels the disappointment cutting through him. "I'm sorry, Father."

Teddy pushes his plate away from him and stews. Mary stands and begins to gather the dishes and says nothing. The tension in the air is heavy. So heavy that mere words couldn't lift it, so silence only feels right. Anna asks to be excused and Mary nods. She begins helping her mother with the cleanup duties. As she comes around the table to take Teddy's plate he stares at her, seething. "Why do you want to see me in trouble so badly?" he asks her, under his breath.

Anna looks at him, and he can see in her face that she does not have an answer. Her mouth becomes a frown, and she sniffles, like she is fighting back tears. "I'm sorry Teddy."

Mary looks over her shoulder and sees the two talking at the table but goes back to what she is doing.

"You begged me to go into the woods to find Ranger, and he is your stupid dog," he hisses at her.

Anna says nothing. The embarrassment on her face shows Teddy all he needs to know.

"Now I'm going to be punished because of you. I hope you're happy," he says, as he scoots his chair back, making it screech against the wooden floor. He walks into the washroom upset. As he is in there, he looks at his face in the reflection and is angry and a little afraid of what his father is going to say to him about this. As he is waiting for the hammer to fall, he hears his father come back into the house.

"Teddy!" Abraham calls out.

Teddy takes in a deep breath, "Yes Father?"

"When you've finished, come outside and help me carry water from the well."

Teddy sighs in relief that he wasn't yelled at, but he remains anxious that the punishment is still coming. He finishes up and makes his way outside.

Chapter Six

Teddy makes his way outside where he sees his father at the well, across the lot. He walks over to meet him, ready to help him, while expecting to be scolded even more now. Abraham is pulling on the rope to retrieve the bucket. At the base of the well, Abraham has already filled two buckets. "Go on son, grab a bucket."

Teddy grabs the handle to the bucket and hoists it from the ground and begins to carry it at his side back to the house. The water sloshes and splashes with each step he takes. He takes it all the way to the house and sets it near the front door. As he makes his way back to the well, his father has already filled another bucket. Teddy waits while his father lowers another. "So…" Abraham begins, "What do you want to tell me?"

"About what?" Teddy retorts.

"Don't be a wise-ass Teddy," Abraham warns, as he lowers the bucket to the bottom of the well. "Tell me why you went into those woods, after I *specifically* told you not to."

Teddy swallows the lump in his throat, "Anna and I were out here playing. We were tossing sticks with Ranger…"

"Go on, boy…" Abraham bites, with a stern tone.

Teddy hesitates, "… Ranger ran into the woods and Anna begged me to go into the woods to find him."

Abraham begins to pull on the rope to retrieve the bucket. "Let me ask you this… Did Anna tell you not to go into the woods, or did I?"

Teddy meets his father's eyes, "You did, sir."

Abraham reaches into the well, grabs the bucket, and pulls it out, placing it onto the ground beside the other three. "So why would you disobey my simple instructions, and listen to your little sister then?"

Teddy grabs another bucket and begins to lug it to the house alongside his father as he considers his response. He feels embarrassed and ashamed that he has disappointed his father and fears how angry he may be, realizing he did outright disobey his instructions, and to make matters worse, he did so less than a day after he was told not to.

"Well? … What do you have to say for yourself?" Abraham asks, carrying a bucket to the house, making much less of a mess than Teddy is with the water.

Teddy stares at the patchy, brown grass, "I thought about what you said last night,"

Abraham slows his pace to match Teddy's, "Alright…"

"You said that I was to be a man soon, and that I would have to protect Anna and Mother," Teddy reminds him. "I just thought…" Teddy stops to avoid sounding nervous and stuttering as he speaks. Every word is very intentional. "Anna was afraid, and she needed me today. I just thought it might be an opportunity to be brave... Like you, Father."

Abraham raises his head to the clouds, maintaining their pace, speechless. After a moment he lets out a sigh, "Teddy, my boy," Abraham begins, with his tone softened. "Perhaps I reacted harshly, out of anger,"

Teddy continues to look at the ground, hanging onto every word, "You told me not to go into the woods, but what you had told me doesn't make sense."

Abraham scrunches his face, not ready to dive into this conversation right now, "Well Teddy, that's because I had not told you everything."

The two drop the buckets next to the front door and make their way back toward the well for the rest. They walk, listening to only the birds in the distance and the uncomfortable silence that lingers in the air. "I saw a woman in the woods today," Teddy says, breaking the uncomfortable silence that hangs in the air.

Abraham's eyes widen, he stops and turns to Teddy, "What!?" Abraham grabs Teddy's shoulders and lowers himself to be eye level. "What else happened? What did you see?" he says, jarring Teddy as he questions him.

"I... I went into the woods looking for Ranger," Teddy begins. "There was a woman, and a cottage."

"The woman, tell me about her."

"Sh- She had Ranger when I found him."

"And he was okay?"

"Yes. But she wouldn't let him go... She told me I shouldn't be in the woods also, and then said I should listen to you." Abraham crouches down, cradling Teddy's face into his hands, shaking… trembling. "Do you know this woman?" Teddy asks.

Abraham stands up and begins to pace short distances, "What else did she say to you? Did she do anything?"

"She told me to run, and then was squeezing Ranger, and I was screaming at her but felt frozen, and that's when I woke up where Anna and Ranger found me." Abraham covers his mouth and rubs his face as he is trying to put the pieces together as he paces. "Who is she, Father?"

Abraham closes his eyes and lets Teddy's curiosity sit with him for a moment. "Very well. What I'm going to tell you is going to sound a bit strange, but I assure you everything I am going to tell you now is true, son."

"You can tell me."

Abraham stares at Teddy with a flat expression while he searches for the words to begin. "You know that I grew up in this house, right?"

"Yes."

"After my parents were gone, I was left with the house and the land it sits on. I figured it'd be easier to keep it than to move your mother, you, and Anna around."

Teddy listens intently, allowing his father to speak openly.

"The story I told you yesterday, about why you can't go into the woods…"

"The one about your friend?"

"Yes, Jack."

"You said you ran out of the woods and Jack wasn't with you."

"This is true… But there is more to the story that is far grislier than I had originally led on," Abraham declares.

"Growing up here, you can imagine I know these woods well, right? So that day we had gone into the woods, playing, like all boys do. We were exploring, only no one told us not to go into the woods. Jack took the lead, and we climbed over sticks and trees, squeezed through bushes, we were having a great time, until we saw a woman." Teddy listens intently, staring at his father who in this moment is treating him like a grown up, and not as a young boy. "The woman, dressed in all black, wore trinkets that I've only heard about. There are said to be women in Salem, just north of here who carry themselves in this way. They call them witches. The town folks would judge them for doing the work of the Devil and stone them to death in public... I'm not sure exactly what it was we saw that day, my memory is fuzzy about the moment still. I remember feeling trapped on my feet. Darkness all around me. Every nerve in my body was fighting to just run away. There I stood, unable to. She wore paint on her pale face, not too much different from the Native Massachusett People we've seen."

"There is no way this could be the same woman, is there? She wore paint on her face as well," Teddy added.

"There is no way to know. I'm not even sure if what I saw was real if I am being honest. I feel crazy when I talk about it. I told people about it when I was younger and no one believed me," Abraham confessed, "so I just stopped talking about it and vowed never to go into the woods again... It's easier sometimes to pretend it never happened."

"What happened to Jack?"

"That is the part that terrifies me to this day," Abraham begins. "I was able to run out of the woods and when I came out, Jack was nowhere to be found. I waited until the sun was going down and I called out to him to no response. Eventually I left. I went home and told my parents. They took me to Jack's parents' house where I told them what had happened. His parents were worried. It was dark. They searched the nearby parts of town and the edge of the woods with no luck. I didn't sleep at all that night… The next day, Jack returned home. Word traveled fast in the town. I was relieved. Everyone was… I felt so guilty. My friend was in trouble. Lost. And I left him alone in the woods. He was probably scared too. I wonder if he had seen the same thing as I had."

"Whatever happened to Jack?" Teddy asks.

Abraham's eyes began to tear up, "I never got a chance to speak to Jack after he came home the following day. I was still trying to make sense of what had happened." Abraham tries to hide his vulnerability, fighting back tears, "I didn't know how to even talk about it after that. So many people looked at me like I was making it up. I felt like everyone took me for being crazier than horseshit. The town watch asked me questions the night it happened and the next day, and after what happened with Jack that following night."

"What happened?" Teddy asks, eager for the end of the story.

"So, Jack comes home, I hear that he isn't quite himself that day. He isn't saying too much to his family or anyone at all. So, the following morning my mother and I were at the market when we heard about what happened from one of the constables who wanted to question me, once more." Abraham picks up one of the buckets and Teddy follows his lead. "Very early that morning Jack was said to have suffocated his younger brother in his sleep. He used a pillow…"

"Do you know where Jack is now?" Teddy asks, lugging the heavy bucket.

"So the way it was told was Jack's father woke up to Jack standing over his mother on the floor, holding a hammer and a chisel. His father was a carpenter, so…"

"So, Jack killed his mother?"

"Jack killed his brother, *and* his mother, and when his father woke up to the horror at his bedside he tried to speak to Jack and Jack just stood there over his mother's body. His father grabbed the chisel and hammer from his hands with no fight… When Jack wasn't responsive, he went to check on his younger son and found him blue in the face in his bed. His father says after he found his son dead that Jack had attacked him and tried to strangle him. His father had scratches on his face and handprints on his neck that left bruises. He killed Jack that morning, fighting for his life while trying to also restrain him. I heard that he slammed his head against the floor many times before fleeing to find help."

Teddy stares at his father, visibly distraught and unsure how to react after hearing that. "That's awful," Teddy says, desperate to fill the awkward silence. "I'm sorry about your friend."

Abraham puts a hand on Teddy's shoulder and squeezes gently, "I suppose it is fine, my boy. I don't know what truly happened, again, these were only the things I had heard over the years. Many years ago, now."

They take the water buckets to the door and go inside. They set the buckets by the hearth for Mary to boil so it can be clean and drinkable. Teddy and Anna then prepare themselves for bedtime, changing into their sleep clothes. The evening is calmer after Abraham spoke with Teddy about the day. Their bond is a little tighter now after has Abraham opened up about what happened with Jack and Teddy's anxiety about his father punishing him seems to have waned significantly. Ranger follows Teddy into the room where Anna is already in bed. Ranger takes his place on the floor between the children's beds.

"Teddy?" Anna says softly.

"What do you want, Anna?"

"I'm sorry that I tattled on you. I feel bad that you got in trouble because of me," she says.

"It's okay... I didn't get in trouble," he says, relieved from his bedside. "Father and I talked about the woods, and I think it best I just don't go there anymore under any circumstance... And you probably shouldn't either."

Mary knocks on the threshold of the door, "Knock knock, are you two ready for sleep?" she asks calmly, with a sweet smile.

"Yes, Mother," Anna replies.

Mary glances over at Teddy, "All ready, Mother," he says to her.

Mary steps into the room and Abraham is behind her. Abraham goes to Anna and hugs her and tucks her in. Mary leans over and kisses her on the forehead and Abraham follows the same. They then go over to Teddy to do the same. Mary sits at his side once he is tucked in and puts her hand gently on his cheek and looks at her precious boy lovingly. "My sweet boy, growing up so fast," she leans forward and kisses him on his forehead. "I love you. Sleep tight," she says as she stands up.

She goes to the door and grabs the lantern from the small table near the door. Abraham walks to the door and he stops for a moment and looks over his shoulder at Teddy. "You didn't actually think you could get away, did you?" Anna and Teddy grin knowing what comes next. Abraham turns around quickly and crouches low with his legs bowed out and his wrists contorted like a monster. "You could never escape *the Tickle*

Monster!" he wails in a guttural, but somehow high-pitched voice. "Gitchy-gitchy-goo, I'm going to tickle you!" he says as he rushes at Anna who kicks her legs and holds her hands out.

"Stop!" she cries. "I don't want you to do that."

Abraham stares at her for a second and he stomps his foot as he pivots to Teddy. "I smell a boy begging for a tickling," he says as he rushes over to Teddy. "Tee-koo! Tee-koo! Tee-koo!" he shrieks as his fingers poke and prod Teddy's ribs, stomach, neck, underarms, and anywhere that Teddy can't protect.

Teddy kicks and squirms, fighting to make it stop. His laughter nearly becomes tears. "Stop, stah- Stop it!"

"I didn't hear *yoooou.*"

"St- … Stop, please! No more!" Teddy stammers, fighting through the laughter as Abraham's fingers hit every sensitive and tender area of flesh that garners a response from Teddy.

Mary stands at the doorway, "That's enough, boys. Your father is done now," she says, shooting a look at Abraham that says more than her words ever could.

Abraham relents and stands up while Teddy catches his breath and adjusts himself again. "Your mother is right. I'm done now,"

"I love you. Sweet dreams," Mary says with her hand on the doorknob.

"Goodnight you two, sleep well." Abraham says. Mary blows out the lantern and pulls the door closed as they turn in for the night.

Chapter Seven

As the children's parents leave the room, the door shuts and the darkness marinates against the hardwood of the floor. It seeps into the corners with shadows cast from the moonlight beaming in from the single window that is between the two beds. There is a blanket setup for Ranger that lays on the floor in the direct moonlight. His paws pitter-patter against the floor, nails scratching as he circles and paces the space trying to get comfortable.

Teddy lies on his back, adjusting his legs to get comfortable. Anna rolls over onto her left side to face Teddy. "Teddy," she whispers.

Teddy turns his head to his right to face her. "Yes?"

"I didn't mean to get you in trouble," Anna whispers, almost too loud to even be a whisper.

"It's okay now," Teddy says with a sigh.

"I'm really sorry," she says.

"Don't worry yourself... Go to sleep now."

Anna rolls over. "Good night," she says, turning to face the wall that her bed sits against with her back to Teddy and the rest of the room.

"Good night, Anna," he replies. Teddy turns over, putting his back to Anna, and faces the other side of the room, as his bed does not sit up against a wall.

Teddy lies on his side under his wool blanket with his eyes closed as he replays the events of the day. What a wild day it has been. The woman in the woods, the blackout, Anna being a rat, the scolding from his mother, and the relief after talking with his father, up until now. His brain picks apart the tragedy of his father's childhood friend Jack and the mention of a woman in the woods. His father described having a lot of the same feelings that he had experienced earlier in the day when he was a boy and went into the woods.

The sound of wind singing in the cool weather outside hums against the house and interrupts the thoughts enough to provoke Teddy to open his eyes. He stares into the void space of the room, submerged with shadows. He hears Anna moving around so he rolls over, "Anna... Are you awake?" he whispers. She doesn't respond and he notices her heavy breathing that is almost a snore. She is clearly out like a smoking candle. He stays laying on his right side now, facing Anna, as he stares at the beam of moonlight that touches the floor and part of the wall near the door. The trees outside cast shadows that dance on the wall to the music of the wind. The branches slither in and out of the light and Teddy lies awake, waiting to fall asleep.

His mind races, and the thoughts scatter like a search party in the woods. After a while he is beginning to fall asleep and with his heavy eyes, fixed on the light shining in on the floor, he sees something move across the wall. It was like a large shadow passing. *Maybe something was outside the window.* His eyes open wide anticipating the movement again. His head raises from his pillow as he stares intently into the light. The room is quiet and there is no more movement. He rests his head again and rolls onto his back where he stares at the ceiling. *It must have been an animal outside or something. Or maybe I'm just tired and starting to see things,* he convinces himself.

Teddy pulls the covers up to his chin and closes his eyes once more and again begins to fall away from wakefulness. From his half-awake state he hears a scuffling noise. It is coming from inside of the bedroom and sounds like it is coming from underneath his bed. It sounds like a fingernail scraping against the wood. He raises up quickly and is startled just as much as he is curious. With his eyes wide open, his heart pounding, and his skin crawling, he tries to focus on the sound over his own breathing. "Anna," he calls out, not whispering this time. She lies still, continuing to lightly snore.

Teddy sits in his bed, scooting his entire body to the head of the bed, pulling the cover over his face, leaving only his eyes and top of his head exposed. He shakes in his bed while Anna sleeps calmly. His eyes shoot around the room from one dark corner to the next. Every paranoid thought disrupts the rhythm of his panicked breathing. He closes his eyes and sinks into his bed with the cover pulled over him completely. The silence is amplified as he focuses on any sound at all. He could hear a mouse outside right now if there were one, as his adrenaline is spiking. Every fiber in his body is screaming that something is wrong.

It is hours later, and Teddy has calmed down a bit and stopped listening so closely at the deafening quiet. His heartbeat is something close to normal and he is as relaxed as he is going to be. He has settled back into a normal sleeping position, lying on his side comfortably after tossing and turning for quite a while. He is starting to feel himself falling asleep when he feels something brush against the bottom of his bare feet. *Was that a fingernail?* Teddy jerks his foot away, bringing his knees close to his chest. He sits up and that is when he hears it. The deep, guttural, almost growling voice of something at the foot of the bed. "Gitchy. Gitchy. Goooooo."

Ranger stands up and is growling just as Teddy feels something tug on the cover but he steals it away, gripping it tight. In that moment there is a sudden shuffling under his bed. He feels something knocking against the underside of where he sleeps. "Mother!" Teddy screams, "Father!" The movement underneath him intensifies, like a deer desperate to escape from a snare. Ranger barks twice and Anna begins to stir, and just as the bedroom door opens, the movement under the bed subsides, and Mary and Abraham come rushing into the room.

Mary lights an oil lantern, "What's the matter, honey?"

Abraham goes to his bedside and sits on his bed. "The tickle monster! It's the tickle monster!" Teddy bellows.

Mary and Abraham's gazes meet, with a mutual look of confusion. "Wh- what do you mean, Teddy?" Mary asks.

"The tickle monster! It tickled my foot! No, it *scratched* my foot! It's in the room!" Teddy cries out, frightened.

"Son, you know that is just a little game we play, right?" Abraham asks, mildly annoyed.

"It was just like when you pretend. I heard it! It said 'gitchy gitchy goo' and everything!" Teddy says.

Mary smiles at him and reaches her arms out to pull him close to her. "Honey, I think you need to relax, could it be-"

Teddy pulls away, "I heard it. I saw its shadow moving around and it was under my bed," Teddy pleads.

Anna sits up in her bed, rubbing her eyes, "What's happening?" she asks.

Abraham goes to her bed and sits beside her. "Nothing is wrong," he pulls the covers up and gestures for her to lay back down. "Try to go back to sleep, dear." Anna lies down as Abraham leans down and kisses her on the cheek and tucks her back in.

"Don't let the tickle monster get me," Teddy begs, looking into his mother's eyes.

Mary pulls him close to her and he rests his head in her arms, against her chest. "Shhhh, it's okay Teddy, my boy." She looks over at Abraham with stern eyes, shaking her head with disapproval. After a moment, Abraham stands up, and Mary lets go of Teddy. "You just lie down now. Try to get some sleep," she says as she leans him back and pulls his covers over him. "I love you," she says as she kisses him on the cheek before she stands up. She joins Abraham at his side by the door, blows out the lantern, and leaves the room with the door open just a little. Ranger gets up and pushes his head through the cracked door and leaves the room. The door sits half-open and now Teddy has to try to go to sleep.

Teddy has lied in bed for what seems like forever since his parents came to check on him when he screamed for them. Terrified and still a little skeptical, he has accepted now that he most likely will never sleep again. How can he? Although he has not heard or seen anything since the bed shaking, whereas his body lies still, his brain soars in all directions, like a scared flock of snowbirds.

With Teddy mostly bored and wide awake, he realizes that he is only fooling himself to think he is getting any sleep at this point. He sits up in his bed and yawns. As he is stretching, he peers into the corners of the room. He wonders what was under his bed. *What did it look like?* Teddy thought again about how he will have to be brave someday, just like his father.

Teddy lays on his stomach and begins to crawl off the side of the bed. He wants to get a good look under the bed before he is able to put his mind at ease. His parents offered him comfort but also sounded like they didn't believe him when he said he had seen the tickle monster. *Seeing is believing,* Teddy thinks, as he creeps off the bed, lowering himself upside down to get a look at what is lurking underneath. As he lowers enough for him to see under the bed, he tenses up, nervous of what he might see. Teddy sighs once he looks under and sees nothing. He only sees the blanket on the floor where Ranger sleeps on the other side, between his and Anna's beds. The deafening silence, the racing thoughts, and self-doubt all collapse onto themselves as Teddy hangs over the side of his bed relieved.

Teddy feels a cool breeze crawl across his skin. With a big exhale, Teddy pulls himself up and suddenly he is in the middle of the woods. He sits upright in his bed that is in the center of a clearing of trees. Surrounded by the woods, he looks around, confused. "Hello?" he calls out. "Anna..." With no answer he listens only to hear the sound of the bare tree branches smacking gently against one another from the wind. As the confusion becomes panic, he looks over the edge of his bed at the ground. Dry dirt, flattened dead leaves, and sticks litter the floor of the woods at his bedside.

With his heart beginning to race, he looks away from the bedside and turns his head to be rattled by a hulking, lumbering shadow, perched at the foot of his bed, leaning over him. With pale white eyes that blink with imperfect synchronization that emanate like stars, it smiles at Teddy. Its smile, a toothy grin made up of a gross underbite from an oversized jaw and a row of large, jagged bottom teeth. The sharp teeth crowd and look unnatural as they point to the heavens and resemble an unstable wrought iron gate. Teddy is frozen, unable to hide his quivering lips and chattering teeth as the scream hides in his chest unable to escape. The smell of this beast is offensive even to a decaying rodent.

The trees around him begin to melt away and the darkness in the room saturates the walls in the bedroom. The dark figure with the milky eyes turns its head sideways, slowly, like Ranger does when he is curious, and with a playful grin, "Tee-koo, tee-koo, tee-koooooo," it growls.

Teddy tries to scoot back when the monster takes a step onto his bed and reveals his arms, held outstretched above his head with contorted elbows. Its massive hands loom high, with long pointy fingers that move merrily as its knuckles nearly scrape the ceiling. Longer fingernails, more akin to claws, wiggle and wriggle toward Teddy, eerily similar to how his father plays when he pretends to be the tickle monster at bedtime. Another step and it is practically standing on top of Teddy now. It tilts its head to the other side and the grin grows wider and the moving fingers stop for a moment.

Time stops for a moment with the only sound to be heard is Teddy's shaky exhales and this thing's croaking. Teddy tries to scream just before the long fingers are jammed into his stomach, like a flash of lightning. "St- Stop!" Teddy struggles to get out, fingernails digging into his flesh. Helpless to ward off this attack, the tears do not take long to follow his cries.

The monster's grin remains plastered, and the tickling becomes less than playful as Teddy's laughter is no more. Only tears and screaming remain. "Tee-koo! ... Tee-koo! ... Tee-koo!" the beast screeches.

Teddy looks over and Anna is still sound asleep in her bed. The door sits opened as it was left. Ranger is nowhere to be found. Mary and Abraham are not bursting in to comfort him like before. "Stop! ... Please! ... No!"

"Teekoo-Teekoo-Teekoo!" it growls, with a high-pitched wail. Teddy hears the rumbling in its stomach between the fits of his own screaming and the monster's terrifying and playful tickling. Helpless to save himself, he is about to surrender to whatever happens. His muscles contract and he curls up against the headboard as the stabbing pains pierce his skin. Teddy sobs, unable to even scream. The monster continues this violent game of tickle monster as its voice fills the dark room. "Tee-koo Tee-koo Tee-koo Tee-koo Tee-koo..."

"Teddy... Teddy... Teddy!" Teddy opens his eyes to his mother, shaking him by his shoulder. He sits up with urgency and looks at his mother's face, and then looks at his body. He inspects himself for cuts and scratches to find nothing.

"Honey, are you feeling okay?" Mary asks.

Teddy looks around the room stunned, putting the pieces together of what was a terrible night. He turns his head, and the sunshine kisses his face. He shields his eyes with the back of his hand quickly, scrunching his face as he does.

"Teddy?" Mary questions, "Are you well?"

'I- I think so," Teddy says with no certainty of his well-being.

"Well, you would be wise to get up, son. You'll sleep half of the day away, lying in bed," Mary says. "Come now, up, up!" she orders, shaking his legs, still under a blanket.

"Yes, Mother," he says. Mary leaves the room and Ranger charges in with his tail wagging. Teddy pulls the cover off and swings his feet to the side of the bed. Ranger rests his head between Teddy's legs and begs to be played with. Teddy hears Anna in the other room singing *Amazing Grace*. She sounds cute singing, but she is getting the words wrong. Mary is heard correcting her and joining in with the singing. Teddy's feet hit the floor with the sun shining in and music in his ears as he tries to start his day right and forget about whatever that nightmare was.

Chapter Eight

Mary spends the later part of the morning cleaning up from the breakfast that Teddy slept through. Teddy has gotten dressed and is sitting at the supper table eating a corn mush cake from the night before. Not long after he finishes, he sits there waiting for Mary to stop what she is doing to help direct him in his studies for the day. Mary is focused on teaching Anna how to dry fruits and vegetables and different ways to preserve them. She sees Teddy watching her move around the hearth and she wipes her hands on her apron. "Anna, honey, why don't you go ahead and try to do some yourself now."

Anna stares at the wooden surface that they are working on and looks at an array of sliced vegetables laid out. "Yes, Mother." Anna picks up the small knife and begins to slice an apple into thin slices.

Mary goes to the table and sits across from Teddy. "Okay, so what are we doing today, son?"

He reaches to the center of the table and grabs a book from a stack of religious books. *Aesop's Fables.* "This one."

Mary takes the book from him and thumbs through it, "Oh, is this the one that your father just gave to you?"

"Yes."

She closes the book and slides it across the table to Teddy, "Well I am sure you are to enjoy this one," she says with a wry smile. "I read this as a girl and I can assure you that it is much more interesting than those," she says with her eyes landing on the small stack of books about Catholicism, Christianity, and Christ.

"You've read this one?" Teddy asks, with a look of doubt on his face.

"Why, sure," she begins, "do you want to know what makes this book particularly interesting?"

He stares at her, curiously.

"The stories in this book… they have a deeper meaning behind them," she explains. "These fables are a sort of way to learn a lesson about life, how to be a decent young man." Mary smiles as she taps the book. "Why don't you go ahead and get started. If you have any questions, write them down and we can talk about them."

Mary gets up and goes back over to Anna where the two of them continue working on the fruits and veggies. Teddy begins to read the book and as time passes he finds himself reading the words on the pages. Although he turns them at a blistering pace, he has no idea what he has just read. He lets out a sigh and does not want to start again. He sits at the table, resting his head in his hand propped up by his elbow. He listens to Anna ask their mother questions about the slab of meat that they are preparing to smoke. Anna is a playful young lady, and her laughter and innocence fills the home with the color of pure joy.

Teddy begins again, starting with the story *The Wolf and His Shadow.* The story is about a wolf who leaves his lair to find food and at the time the sun casts his shadow far out onto the ground making him seem much bigger than he truly is. The wolf admired his shadow and thought that it was silly that he should have to run from a lion and that there was no reason he shouldn't be king. As the wolf stood there, an even bigger shadow consumed his own shadow and before he knew it the lion appeared and struck him down with a single blow.

While reading that story, Teddy is reminded of the shadows that danced along the wall the night before in their room. He tries to move onto the next page but now is overcome with the fear he had in his dream last night. The dream that did not feel like a dream at all. It felt more like a nightmare, but even then was more vivid and present in his mind. Teddy would typically forget his dreams not long after. He would remember that he dreamt but as he began to share the dream, he would learn that the details were a little fuzzy and before long would become nothing more than an afterthought. But this was not the same. He remembered everything so vividly. He remembers the smell of his pillow when he would put it to his face. The strange and dizzy feeling of hanging upside down to look under the bed.

Mary glances at Teddy who sits at the table with the book open, but he is spaced out staring at the front door.

"Thinking of heading off somewhere?" Mary asks with a grin. Teddy does not respond. Mary puts a hand on Anna's back, "Anna, sweetheart, won't you go to the garden and gather some fresh peas?"

Anna dusts off her hands, "Yes, Mother."

She slips her shoes on, "Come on Ranger!" she says as Ranger hurries to the door with his tail wagging and his tongue panting.

Mary goes over to the table and has a seat across from Teddy. "What is on your mind, dear?"

Teddy breaks his concentration, staring into nothing, "Huh?"

"How is the book, dear?"

"Uh, it's ...fine, I guess."

Mary stares at him with an eyebrow raised. "You seem a bit distracted... Is something troubling you?"

Teddy looks into her eyes from across the table, tapping his finger on the tabletop. "Did you and Father come into our room last night?"

Mary's suspicion quickly turns to confusion, "Yes, after you screamed for us."

Teddy's face turned to horror as he felt his stomach sink. "So, it was real?"

"What was real?" she asked.

"Did I tell you what I saw? Last night."

"You had told us something was in your room, but you were hysterical. Your father and I couldn't make any sense of anything you were saying."

"So, it wasn't a dream," Teddy says aloud to himself, enough for Mary to hear him.

"Teddy, what is going on?"

"Don't think I'm crazy. Last night was real, I think. I spent the entire night unable to sleep, completely terrified in bed. I woke up this morning though and wasn't sure that it was not a dream."

"Teddy, there is no way anything was in your room though. Your father and I checked. You were just having night terrors," she says dismissively.

"No! I saw it! It-It's big hands. It's claw digging into me when it was tickling me! I couldn't move! It wouldn't stop! …And, and I was bleeding!"

"Teddy, we checked on you after and you were sound asleep,"

This doesn't make any sense, Teddy thinks. Now he is having an internal crisis because he doesn't know when he fell asleep and what was real or a dream.

"When did you check on me?"

"Teddy, please-"

"No! Listen to me! It had- It had big… *big* white eyes. A row of jagged teeth. Its breath was putrid!" Teddy expresses with certainty.

"Teddy… Maybe we should wait for your father to–"

"You don't believe me!" Teddy accuses. He stands up and goes to a shelf across the room and grabs an envelope and a stick of coal. "I will show you!" he blurts out.

Mary rests her head in her hand, "Teddy…"

Teddy begins to scribble and sketch on the back of the stained envelope with what he remembers this thing looking like. As he is working on his *proof,* the front door opens and Ranger rushes inside before Anna. Ranger runs up to Teddy's side, throwing his front paws into Teddy's lap as he tries to work.

"I didn't quite fill up the basket, but I got a lot, Mother," Anna says proudly, as she kicks the door shut with the ball of her foot and a basket on her arm.

"Set it by the hearth please," Mary says.

Anna sets the basket near the other foods and takes her coat off. "What are you two doing?" Anna asks as she sees Mary looking aggravated and Teddy scribbling obsessively. She stands beside where Teddy is sitting. "What are you drawing, Teddy?" Teddy ignores her as he focuses on the lines. Anna looks at her mother, "Mother, what is he doing?"

"Teddy is showing us what he saw in his dream last night–"

"Not a dream! It was real!" he hisses, as he uses his hand to brush away, smearing loose chunks of messy coal powder from the drawing. He picks it up and studies it for a moment before presenting it to Mary.

That afternoon, Abraham returns home. He goes about his normal ritual of coming home, greeting everyone, taking care of small things outside with the animals, and then comes inside once Mary announces that supper is ready. Abraham comes inside and takes his seat. The children ask for permission to be seated and Mary takes her seat. They join hands and say a prayer before the meal as the dishes make their way around the table.

"Anna, honey, why don't you tell your father about the apples?" Mary starts.

Anna finishes chewing her food, "Mother showed me how to dry apple slices!"

"Oh, that sounds wonderful, I love apples," Abraham replies, with an impressed look on his face just before he takes a bite of food.

"And Teddy started his new book today," Mary says while she looks at Teddy as he pushes his peas around his plate with no urgency to eat.

"Oh yeah? The book that I got him?" Abraham asks as he shoots a glance over at Teddy.

"Yes, the one with the parables," Mary tells him.

Abraham nods as he chews another bite. "So… What have you read so far, son?"

Teddy plays with his food, knocking around the different vegetables with the prongs of his fork. "I read about the Tortoise and the Hare, The Lion and the Mouse, and the Wolf and the Shadow," he says.

"Those are all great," Abraham says, still chewing, unable to withhold his interest. "Mmm, have you read about The Fox, The Cock, and The Dog yet?"

"No, sir."

"That is one of my favorites, you should look for that one."

Mary watches Teddy, as he seems less engaged than normal as he picks at his food. "Teddy, dear... You've not touched your food."

Teddy's eyes look up, but his head doesn't move as he continues to slowly spin the fork on his plate. "I'm not hungry."

"Teddy, did you show Father your drawing?" Anna asks with glee.

Teddy locks eyes with Abraham just before Abraham looks at Mary who sighs, putting her fork down. "Drawing?" Abraham asks. "Let's see it!"

Mary reluctantly gets up and goes to retrieve the drawing. She brings it over to Abraham and slides it in front of him, face down on the table. He stares at it for a moment as he leans back in his chair. "What am I looking at here?" he asks, picking it up and turning it over to see the deep black figure that Teddy swears is the Tickle Monster.

"Teddy drew a monster. Do you like it?" Anna asks, poorly reading the energy of the room.

Abraham looks at Teddy, "What is this, son?" he asks, looking over at Mary for answers.

Teddy puts his fork down and drops his hands into his lap. "It's the Tickle Monster," he says, with his voice lower than his head.

Abraham shakes his head, staring at the envelope, "I see." The silence hangs heavy in the air before Mary starts taking away dishes of food. The metal clinks against ceramic breaking the silence. Ranger's tail wags, knocking against the table leg as he begs for food at Anna's tableside.

"If you two are finished you may be excused," Mary says to Anna and Teddy. Anna sits and continues to eat, oblivious to the mood switch at the table. Teddy pushes his plate away from him and leaves the table. Mary continues to clean up while Anna and Abraham finish their meals in silence.

After supper, the family goes to their typical chores. Anna helps Mary clean up the house while Teddy and Abraham go outside and draw water from the well, bring wood inside, and make sure the chickens are inside of their coop. The goat is comfortable under shelter with plenty of hay. There is a cold front coming through tonight and it has already begun to snow early into the evening. The overcast sky can only be seen through the snowfall.

After the evening chores, Anna and Teddy wash up and change into their bedtime clothes. Teddy is tired after the long day he has had. The night before has weighed heavy on his mind, and he feels insane when he tries to talk about it. *How can they not believe me? Why would I lie?* he wonders. *Is this how Father felt when they were looking for Jack?* Teddy lies down in his bed quietly. Anna comes in shortly after him as Ranger gallops in, circling her feet before she hops in her bed.

"Ranger! Stop it, boy!" she cries out, with laughter laced in her voice. Ranger climbs up and licks her face and is not quite ready for sleep. "Teddy, get Ranger!" she begs with a smile that shows all her teeth. Teddy ignores her as he lies there just waiting for the lantern to be blown out. Anna's laughter fills the house as her face scrunches up trying to hold Ranger at bay. "*Noooo* Ranger, go get Teddy. Teddy wants to play now.*"

Ranger turns and drops to the floor and jumps on Teddy's bed. He licks Teddy, who turns away and puts his hand on the back of Ranger's head and pets him softly, and scratches behind his ears. "Not right now boy, come on, let's get down," Teddy says. Ranger climbs off the bed and stands on the wood floor between the two children's beds. His nails clack against the wood with each movement.

Mary and Abraham make their way into the bedroom, as they do routinely every night. Mary sits at Teddy's bedside while Abraham sits with Anna. Abraham holds her hand as she lies comfortably on her pillow staring at her father with a thin-lipped smile. "What are you going to make tomorrow with your mother?" he asks as he caresses her small hand in his.

"Um, carrots and apples."

"Mmmm, I love apples. Has she shown you how to peel potatoes?"

"Yes," Anna replies with her teeth showing.

Mary stares at Teddy, lovingly, as he stares at her growing more uncomfortable each second. "What is it?" he asks.

She places her hand on his chest, "I hope you have a good night of rest tonight, dear. Better than last night. Tomorrow will be a better day."

"I will try Mother," he says.

Mary kisses him on the cheek and he puts his arms around her and they hug. "I love you Teddy… Goodnight."

As she gets up, Abraham and her switch beds. Mary is telling Anna good night and they are talking about what they are going to be doing tomorrow. Abraham sits at Teddy's side, "You planning to read more of those fables tomorrow?" he asks.

"Yes, sir," Teddy answers.

"Alright, well make sure you get a good night's rest, son." Abraham kisses him on the forehead and hugs him before standing up. "Make sure you come and get us if you need to, alright?"

Teddy nods his head, agreeing. Abraham stands at Mary's side as she tucks Anna in and kisses her goodnight. Mary stands up and gives another look at Teddy and back to Anna as the parents stand at the door. Mary picks up the lantern from the small table by the door. "Goodnight you two," Mary whispers.

Abraham stops for a moment and stares at Anna who begins to grin and tense up. He crouches down and raises his arms in the air, "You guys didn't think you would get-"

Mary nudges him, "That's enough. Not tonight, Abraham," she says assertively.

Teddy looks unamused. Abraham stands up straight and clears his throat. "We love you. Sweet dreams," he says.

Mary blows out the lantern and walks out of the room and Abraham pulls the door closed as they leave the children to get their rest.

Chapter Nine

The door closes and the darkness is ever present, even more-so than the previous night. The house is warm from the wood burning in the hearth as smoke billows from the small chimney, but the bedroom is not as cozy. Teddy curls up in his bed and pulls the cover over most of his body to keep warm. Anna employs a similar strategy in her bed. Teddy lies there with his eyes closed giving it his best effort to get a full night of sleep, as he is already exhausted. The wind beats against the house while snowflakes kiss the plate glass. The wood creaks and cracks under the wind outside.

Teddy tosses and turns, finding it quite difficult to get comfortable. Listening to the winter breathing outside has him anticipating a hard day of work tomorrow. Anna begins to stir a bit, "Lay still, Teddy," she groans.

Teddy's eyes open. "I'm sorry. I'm just trying to get comfortable."

The two lay quiet and still for a moment before Anna starts to toss and turn. "How far does Father have to ride in the morning to work?" she asks.

Teddy turns over onto his side and faces her, "I'm not sure really. Miles."

The wind outside continues to hum while they lay. "Teddy?" she asks.

"Yes?"

"Tell me about the stories you're reading."

"...Go to sleep Anna."

"Pleeeease," she begs.

"I suppose they are short. I could tell you one," he offers.

Anna turns onto her side, facing Teddy. "Do you have a favorite? Will you tell me?"

"I've only read a few," he whispers with disappointment in his voice. "But I can tell you the one about the brother and the sister."

Anna props herself up on her elbow with her head raised. "There was a man who had two children, a boy and a girl. The boy thought of himself quite handsome. His little sister, ugly. Hideous really. Much like you," Teddy began with a jab of sibling cruelty. The smile sits on his face, the first time he has smiled all day it feels like.

Anna giggles, "Stop it, Teddy, tell it right!"

"I am!" he laughs. "...So, the two are playing when the boy catches his reflection in the looking glass. The sister looks at herself, and she doesn't look as pretty."

Suddenly Anna's face becomes serious. "Are you just making this up?"

Teddy smirks, "I promise this is a real story."

"So, what happened?" she asks, still suspicious that this may be a playful ruse by her older brother.

"Their father comes along, and the brother starts to brag about how much more handsome he is than her…" Anna gasps, annoyed. Teddy smiles, unable to contain himself, "I'm not joking! I can show you!"

"Go on then," she orders.

"So, the father looks at the boy and tells him that he would be well to not ruin his looks by being angry and to not be so vain. Then he looked at the sister and told her that she would be best to make up for her ugly face, *that looks like yours*, and be kind and sweet and speak well."

"Is that it?" she asks, with a flat expression.

Teddy rolls onto his back with a long exhale. "Yes."

"Well, that doesn't seem like much of a story," she says, as she lies her head back onto her pillow.

"Most of the stories are only a page or two from what I can tell."

They lay for a moment longer as the wind outside seems to be really picking up now. "Can I ask you something?" Anna asks in a sweet voice.

"Sure, what is it?"

"Can you teach me to read?"

Teddy turns his head to the ceiling. "I suppose I could try to."

"Is it hard?" she asks.

"Only at first," Teddy tells her, "But once you start to figure it out, it is really easy."

"I will talk to Mother about seeing if I can read with you, maybe."

Teddy pulls the covers over his shoulders and finds a comfortable position to lay. "Sure, Anna... Go to sleep now."

"I love you big brother, goodnight," Anna says as she rolls over, with her back to Teddy and her face close to the wall.

"Goodnight," Teddy says softly.

The time passes into the late night and the children have fallen asleep now. The snow outside has only intensified, and Teddy wakes up from the cold. His teeth chatter and his bones shake as he tries to fix the cover to his body more. He curls his knees and brings them close to his chest to make himself a ball of heat. Ranger raises his head up and sees Teddy moving around. "Come here boy," Teddy says, waving for Ranger. Ranger hops onto the bed and the two lay together close. Teddy is unable to sleep. The chill has an icy grip on him and cozying up to the dog is not making it much better like he had hoped.

Teddy lies there listening to the winter outside while he watches the moonlight shining into the room. The snow flurries outside cast small shadows onto the wall and part of the floor and as Teddy fixates on the light it begins to look like reflections from moving water. As he is focusing on the moonlight in the room, the light is broken by a shadow that passes through the light quickly. If you were to blink, you might miss it. Teddy raises up immediately. Ranger raises up as well and hops down from the bed.

"Anna..." Teddy whispers. She stirs slightly before going still again. "Anna, are you awake?" Teddy asks, this time a little louder than a whisper.

Anna pulls her knees closer to her chest and pulls the cover closer to her face, "Teddy, I am trying to sleep." she huffs.

"Anna, it's back," he says quietly, as if he is trying not to let the shadow hear him warning her. "Anna…"

Anna does not respond and now Teddy's heart rate is beginning to increase. He can feel his heartbeat thrumming in his ears. His breathing becomes heavier, like it might sound before someone cries. He peers into the light with snowy shadows moving in the moonlight trying to calm himself when he hears the scuffling and scratching noises again. The noise is coming from the dark corner furthest away from the light on the floor. He turns to investigate the corner and his eyes do not adjust to the dark, but instead the room becomes darker as if his natural sense to adapt to darkness has all but fled his senses. As he watches the corner and feels the darkness creeping in around him, he hears the sounds again, only this time they are coming from beneath Anna's bed.

His head jerks toward her bed, like his neck is on a wound spring being released. The darkness, overwhelming, threatens to swallow the moonlight while Anna lays still as a rock, and quiet as a mouse. He hears his own breathing and Ranger pacing now, with his nails scratching against the floor. "Shhh, Ranger, sit!" he commands. The wind continues battering the outside of the cottage and the window rattles gently. Teddy's eyes shoot from corner to corner, then corner to Anna's bed. He stares into the crevice underneath her bed. Just big enough to crawl under if he needed to. It is even darker as he stares into the deep blackness under his little sister's bed. He thinks about the lion's shadow overwhelming the wolf's shadow in the story and then out of the corner of his eye he sees, no, he *feels* the shadow pass over the moonlight that hugs the floor.

The movement from his peripheral was just enough to provoke a scream from him. "Mother! Father! Come, come! It's back! It's back!" he cries out.

The bedroom door swings open, and Mary comes bursting into the room with a lantern, not lit yet. "Honey, what is it?" she asks, calmly while trying to light the flame. Abraham is right behind her.

"The shadows. They're moving again!" Teddy howls.

"Are you sure it wasn't just something outside, son?" his father asks through a powerful yawn.

"It's not. It's a big shadow. And there were noises underneath Anna's bed, I swear!" Teddy pleads.

Abraham takes the lantern from Mary, and she has a seat beside Teddy, pulling his head into her chest where he rests against her heartbeat while she strokes his hair. Abraham sets the lantern on the floor and gets on his hands and knees and looks under the bed, scooting the lantern closer to the bed frame to illuminate underneath. "There is nothing under the bed, Teddy," he says as he raises back to his feet. Ranger stands on all fours and is curious what is happening.

"It was there, I'm telling you, it was there," Teddy says between big breaths.

Anna begins to stir and rolls over to see her father standing there with the lantern and her mother consoling Teddy. "What's going on?" she asks, half awake.

"Nothing, dear. Go back to sleep," Abraham says as he touches her face and kisses her on the forehead. She lies back down and pulls the cover to her chin and closes her eyes. After a short while, Mary whispers to Teddy, "Are you okay to go back to sleep now?"

Teddy pulls his arms from around her and lays his head back on his pillow. "I can try."

"Alright, holler if you need me. We will be right in here," she assures him. Teddy pulls the covers over himself, getting comfortable as Mary rises to her feet. Abraham stands in the doorway and leaves the lantern on the table with the flame going and Mary follows behind him. Ranger follows them out as well.

"Mother," Teddy says.

"Yes, dear?"

"Can you leave the door open a bit?" he asks with the dread still present in his voice.

"Of course," she says as she leaves the door cracked, half-opened.

Chapter Ten

Teddy watches every dark corner and sneaky crevice, suspicious of something more insidious. He feels as if the cracks between the floorboards and the hiding spots he normally doesn't think about are watching him. They are surely alive; he just knows it. Every gust against the house and cracking of the house settling in the cold is sure to be the symphony of his undoing tonight.

After a while, Teddy starts to slip into the state of being half-asleep and half-awake. As he is falling away, he hears the pitter patter sounds across the floor. His eyes shoot open, and he raises up alarmed and immediately sees nothing. "Ranger... Ranger, is that you buddy?" he murmurs. He hears Ranger get up in the other room and stroll into the bedroom, brushing against the door with his head to open it even more. The sound of his nails is not the same noise Teddy woke up to though. Ranger stands at Teddy's bedside panting with his tail wagging slowly.

Teddy reaches out and rubs his head and Ranger licks his forearm as he does. "Ranger, go on back to sleep, buddy."

Ranger turns and goes back out of the room. Anna still lies still, completely unmoved by the commotion. Teddy closes his eyes and as he gets comfortable and begins to slip away, into sleep, he is once again awakened by a loud slam. He sits up quickly, and sees the door is closed and now Ranger is outside of the door and has begun barking. Teddy pops back up with his blood pumping now and his heart drumming within his chest. He stares at the door and then looks at Anna. She is beginning to stir but still seems mostly undisturbed. He turns back to the door and that is when the small flame from the oil lantern on the desk near the door goes out. Teddy's imagination is assembling the pieces to his perfect nightmare right from the comfort of his bed. He looks over at Anna and now she is gone from her bed, only her blanket and pillow left thrashed.

"Anna!" he calls out, to no reply. The wind outside mocks him as the snow accumulates on the outside windowsill. The onset of winter in Cambridge has chilled the home while the shadows dancing in the room have chilled his blood. Teddy looks around the room for Anna while Ranger barks outside of the bedroom door. He looks around the room just short of panicking. To his left, nothing, then to his right, nothing, and then he hears it.

"Teekoo, teekoo," in a voice that sounds like several voices at once in various pitches. His eyes follow the sound, and he looks up and sees Anna on the ceiling facing down while her hands and feet lay flat. Her limbs are contorted and look very unnatural as she stays there, suspended. Her white eyes peer through the strands of hair that hang over her face.

"Anna! What- what are you doing, Anna?"

Anna's head snaps to her right as her arms and legs scamper backwards like a skittering bug with a million little legs. She glides across the ceiling and down the wall near the door and falls to the floor before she recovers and hides in the dark corner of the room, farthest from the window. The shadows in the room engulf her entirely, making it difficult for Teddy to see her, until eventually he cannot see her at all. "Mother!" he screams. "Come quick! Something is the matter with Anna!" There is a thud on the floor and Teddy's labored breathing only magnifies his rising fear.

He scoots up to the head of his bed with his knees to his chest when he feels something tugging on his blanket, trying to pull it away from him. He grips the blanket tight and looks to the foot of the bed and sees an arm swing up from the floor and a hand slam onto the bed, gripping the topside of the blanket tight. It is Anna's arm. She pulls herself from the floor with one arm before she awkwardly slams her other arm onto the blanket with a windmilling, over-the-top swing. She pulls herself onto the top of the bed and now is in a crouched position, perched on the footboard.

Teddy draws his feet back even more. "Mother!" he calls out, as Ranger continues to bark outside. "Father!" No answer. No parents bursting through the door with warm light and forehead kisses. "What are you doing, Anna!?" Anna tilts her head to her right side slowly, her face hidden by her hair, and a soft growl that feels like a vibration in Teddy's ears as he watches her. A vibration that creeps into his bones and makes him tremble.

Anna raises her head up and the moonlight in the room barely misses her but is enough to reveal that this is not Anna. Something is wrong as Teddy sees her face. "Anna! Stop it! I don't like this!" Her face resembles the face from the monster he had seen the night before. "Mother! Father!" he calls out. Milky white eyes pierce through his soul, and an unsettling blink breaks the stare. One eye blinks while the other is a gasp slower. The eyes aren't quite moving simultaneously. She snaps her head back into an upright position and Teddy hears the bone and cartilage popping and tearing. Her mouth opens wide revealing large bottom teeth that become more visible when she unhinges her jaw and pulls it out to create a massive underbite. Sharp, jagged, and pointy teeth that do not match her mouth at all hide her upper lip.

"Gitchy gitchy gooooo," she growls, in a guttural tone, "I'm gonna get you." Teddy knows what comes next if this is anything like the night before with the shadow figure. He does not plan to stick around and find out if it plays out the same. Anna takes a step toward him, and he jumps off the bed. His feet hit the floor and he slips and slides trying to gain balance. Anna rolls off the bed to the floor, reaching for his feet, "Teekoo teekoo!"

Teddy swings the door open, and his mother and father are standing there. Ranger stands on his hind legs barking aggressively and showing teeth. "Teddy! Wh-" Mary says as Teddy runs out of the room past her, nearly knocking into her. Ranger chases Teddy and Anna runs out of the room after Teddy. He opens the front door and races outside, into the undisturbed, fresh white snow. He rushes into the night as the cold air clutches onto him. His heavy breathing, now visible with each big exhale, like a warning that he should have grabbed his coat like his mother tells him to everytime he leaves the house.

"Teddy! Wait!" He hears Anna holler for him as she runs after him. Chasing him still he charges through the snow, unable to move fast enough. Ranger follows him out the door in a hurry.

He looks back and sees her coming faster, she is closing in. He sees the stump where his father and he cut wood on a regular basis. The ax handle stands raised, ready to grab, with the head planted into the flat surface of the tree stump. Covered in snow, Teddy recognizes the shape just fine. Completely overtaken by fear, and overtaken by the need to be brave, to be a man like his parents want. He does not want to disappoint them as he knows he will need to protect them all, and how can he protect *them* if he cannot protect himself?

Teddy slows his pace and stops at the stump. He grabs the handle, not bothering to brush off the snow, and he plants a foot against the side of the tree and pulls the ax free. With no time to waste, he remembers what his father taught him recently of how to properly swing an ax. With complete disregard of technique, he drags the ax from the ground and swings it like a sword, cutting through the night and snowfall, and makes an immediate impact.

He steps back with his eyes wide, horrified. He lets go of the ax and it sticks out of Anna's small chest. She looks into Teddy's eyes, no longer being the host of those terrifying features he had seen only moments ago. She falls to her knees and collapses into the snow. "Anna! No!" Mary screams, dashing to them and lifting Anna's head from the snow and inspecting the wound in her chest. "No no no no no!" she cries, holding Anna's head against her chest. "What have you done!?" she shrieks, staring daggers through Teddy.

Anna's body goes lifeless before Abraham catches up to them. "Oh God! Son! What the hell did you do!?" He falls to his knees and pulls Anna from Mary. "No, Anna!" He smacks her cheeks as if she is only sleeping. "Anna!" The blood spills from her chest wound. Abraham pulls the ax from her chest and tosses it across the property. "Anna! … Anna!" he howls. Abraham gently rests her in Mary's arms as she weeps. Abraham stomps over to Teddy with rage written on his face. "What did you do!?" he shouts, as Teddy backs away, afraid of his father. "Why!?" Abraham shouts as he stands over Teddy who stumbles onto his bottom in the snow, "That was your little sister, Teddy!" He crouches down with his face cradled into his hands before letting go and exploding back up. "You were supposed to protect her!"

Teddy unleashes a river of tears as he struggles to speak. He scoots backwards as his father stalks toward him, "I- it..."

"What!?" Abraham interrupts, shouting angrily.

"It was the tickle monster…" Teddy pleads, with tears streaming down his cold cheeks.

Abraham collapses into the snow on his hands and knees and begins to weep. He cries in a way that Teddy has never seen his father do before. He has never seen his father cry, ever. Teddy looks past Abraham and sees his mother shattered, still holding Anna's body as she cries out for the coming morning to hear her heart breaking.

"She was the tickle monster... I killed the tickle monster…" Teddy says aloud, more to convince himself than anyone else. Teddy sees Anna in his mother's arms, the front of her clothes soaked in a deep, deep red that had begun to saturate the snow. Teddy's fear of what is trying to get him dissipates but is replaced by the fear of what he has done. "I killed the tickle monster," he says with uncertainty before his voice is broken by the oncoming urge to cry. "I… I Killed… I *killed* her."

Abraham crawls over beside Mary, shuffling through the snow and hard ground as he cries harder at the sight of Anna.

"Please, wake up sweetie!" Mary begs. She rocks back and forth while Abraham wraps his arms around her. Tears stream down his face and he looks away from Anna. He weeps, completely destroyed.

Teddy stands up, in disbelief of what is happening. His feet carry him away involuntarily with the house at his back. All he hears is his own labored breathing and wailing from his parents. The cold air has no effect on him with everything that has just happened. He runs as fast as he can with no destination in mind. No plan to follow. He just knows he can't deal with seeing his parents break. The way his father looked at him was enough to break any child's heart. He runs farther away, not believing that he killed his sister.

Abraham sits in the snow, knees buried beside his wife and daughter. He squeezes her tight, never wanting to let her go as the realization grabs hold of him that this is the last time he will see his sweet, sweet Anna above ground. He lets go, unleashing a wild flurry of emotions. Tears break through, crashing into the snow as he rests his chin on Mary's shoulder. A broken woman under the stars, she hangs her head, clutching Anna's lifeless body. She raises her head and looks out to the distance through watery eyes to see Teddy running away.

Abraham's eyes peel open from intense straining. He looks out across the pasture that stretches from the side of the house all the way to the woods. The moonlight shines down making the undisturbed, fresh white snow on top of the grass glow. The white is almost blinding at night. His eyes focus on the tree lines and how the silhouette of the trees rest against the horizon. He gazes into the woods with his wife in his arms as he notices something. Movement. He pulls away from Mary and rises to his feet. He wipes his eyes and steps forward. Off in the distance, where the trees begin, he sees a person.

"Abraham," Mary calls out. "Where are you going?"

Abraham doesn't answer her while he continues to stride forward, bare feet shuffling in the snow. Upon a better look, he sees that it is a woman in all black. She stands at the base of the trees, staring back at Abraham. The surge of cold that massages his spine and gives him gooseflesh also provides a sinking feeling in his gut. The same feeling that pairs well with making the hair on the back of his neck stand up. The same familiar feeling he had as a teenager in these very woods. Abraham is immobilized in the middle of the pasture.

"Abraham... What are you doing?" Mary screams through a ragged voice.

Abraham is enamored with the woman, but physically incapable of moving. Their eyes are locked with some distance between them. She turns her body toward the trees, maintaining eye contact until her head turns. The woman in all black fades into the trees, out of sight. Abraham's knees go weak, and he collapses. Afraid, confused, and defeated, he is left to sort through what remains of this family.

THE END

Acknowledgements

This story began as somewhat of a joke in my household over the years prior to writing this. When my youngest son was much smaller, like most fathers and sons, we would wrestle and play and eventually it would turn into me tickling him. Like most rough-housing and tickle-fights, eventually I don't know when to stop, and he doesn't have fun anymore. Suddenly, dad becomes the tickle monster. I would get into character and stomp around the house, with a very fast and creepy walk, and a kind of goofy voice that I always imagined would be creepy in the right setting.

As he got older this became more of me just trying to be funny and take it a little *too far*. I started joking when we would play that one day, he is going to feel very silly when he sees I wrote a book, and this is me continuing to take this just a little *too far*. What you've just read is an inside joke that I took way too far. I don't know what is wrong with me or why I am like this, but I don't think I should stop now.

Aidyn

I want to give a special thanks first and foremost to my son, Aidyn. You've always been a lit fuse but also have such an imaginative excitement that as I get older, I wish I could just capture a fraction of it. Listening to you be excited about *anything* is fascinating at times and I am happy to share this small, silly game we played together. I love you, and I hope you like this story and that it is special to you to have been involved in the inception of …The Tickle Monster.

Kaylynn

A special thanks to my lady, Kaylynn, who edits my gibberish and helps catch my oversights. She does well to tell me when commas should be periods and when periods should be commas. She also hears the infancy of my stories long before they make much sense. This story is an example of that.

My Advanced Readers

Your insight, reactions, and callouts to my work is always nerve-racking as I anticipate, but the insight is always so valuable for the reader's experience. One of my favorite things about being a writer has been the constant learning on the job. A super special shout-out (not your ordinary *regular* shout-out) to these people who showed up for me when called upon and gave great feedback and called me on my nonsense. I'm still a little surprised anyone wants to read what I write sometimes, so thank you, one hundred times. This story is tightened up and made much better with your comments.

Ali Athanasiou * A.W. Mason * Becky Howard *
Frank Wurzelbacher * Kiana Hawley * Nadine Stewart *
Nikki Kossaris * Shaun AIC Wilson * Todd Condit *
Torrence Bryan * Willie G. Heredia *

You

Thank you for choosing to spend your time reading this short story. I hope you enjoyed reading it as much as I enjoyed conceptualizing it. Researching the Colonial times in America was much more of an undertaking than I originally had expected but once I was digging in, it was too late to turn back. I had a lot of fun reading up on it! When you find yourself googling "What is mush cake?" you know you've got an exciting story on your hands. With all sincerity though, thank you!

If you enjoyed this story, I would like to invite you to rate and review this title on Amazon, Goodreads, and anywhere else that this book may be available.

Also, please tag me on social media if you share the things you read. I would love to hear from you.

@WASHBURNWRITES

About The Author

David Washburn is a father and a boyfriend residing in a house on the west side of Cincinnati. With two teen boys who are left to their own devices he finds he has more time to himself to write books like this or toy with any other hobbies or bright ideas. David is the most routine person on earth (and certain that his predictability will be his downfall someday) so if he isn't at the gym trying to bust out of his skin, he is at home reading or watching *too much* TV.

David's writing is heavily influenced by a lifetime fandom of horror movies and violent music. David is creatively driven by grounded, rational thinking that is strangled by anxiety that wears the mask of an overactive imagination. At the time of this book's publishing, he is a self-publishing author.

www.ingramcontent.com/pod-product-compliance
Lightning Source LLC
Chambersburg PA
CBHW031853170626
46807CB00004B/1699